WHO?

Algirdas Jonas Budrys, a Lithuanian citizen, was
born in Königsberg, East Prussia, in 1931
and brought up in the United States. His father
is Consul General for Lithuania in New York
City. He says of himself: 'I have seen Adolf
Hitler, Henry Wallace, Franklin Roosevelt, and
Douglas MacArthur stimulate crowds at
which I stood by. I have shaken Harry Truman's
hand. I have seen the *Graf Zeppelin* and the
Hindenburg float over Königsberg in majestic
company; I have seen the swastika-chalked brick-
halves that came through our windows at night,
and I was playing in a sandbox in Manhattan
the afternoon the *Hindenburg* cruised overhead
on the way to a thunderstorm and her grave.
I have been called a Nazi, a Communist, a clod, a
petit bourgeois, and a long-haired egghead.
I am, in short, a child of the twentieth century.'

Algis Budrys has held a number of jobs, such
as labourer, restaurant counterman, and film
theatre doorman. He sold his first fiction in 1952,
and was an editorial assistant at Gnome Press,
Galaxy Magazine, and *Space Science Fiction* in
1952–3. He went on to be Associate Editor
of *Venture Science Fiction* and the *Magazine of
Fantasy and Science Fiction* in 1957, became
a free-lance editorial consultant, and then, in
1961, Editor-in-Chief of Regency Books.
Since 1963 he has been Editorial Director of the
Book Division of the Playboy Press. Among his
other books are; *False Night, Man of Earth, The
Falling Torch, The Unexpected Dimension,
Rogue Moon,* and *The Furious Future.*

Algis Budrys

WHO?

Penguin Books

Penguin Books Ltd, Harmondsworth,
Middlesex, England
Penguin Books Pty Ltd, Ringwood,
Victoria, Australia

First published in the USA 1958
Published in Great Britain by Gollancz 1962
Published in Penguin Books 1964
Copyright © Almat Publishing Corp. 1958

Made and printed in Great Britain by
C. Nicholls & Company Ltd
Set in Intertype Times

*This book has been dedicated all along to
Frank Kelly Freas, who first created Martino,
and to Walter Fultz, who saw him last*

Chapter 1

It was near the middle of the night. The wind came up from the river, moaning under the filigreed iron bridges, and the weathercocks on the dark old buildings pointed their heads north.

The Military Police sergeant in charge had lined up his receiving squad on either side of the cobbled street. Blocking the street was a weathered concrete gateway with a black-and-white striped wooden rail. The headlights of the M.P. super-jeeps and of the waiting Allied Nations Government sedan glinted from the raised shatterproof riot visors on the squad's varnished helmets. Over their heads was a sign, fluorescing in the lights:

YOU ARE LEAVING THE ALLIED SPHERE

YOU ARE ENTERING THE SOVIET SOCIALIST SPHERE

In the parked sedan, Shawn Rogers sat waiting with a man from the A.N.G. Foreign Ministry beside him. Rogers was Security Chief for this sector of the A.N.G. administered Central European Frontier District. He waited patiently, his light green eyes brooding in the dark.

The Foreign Ministry representative looked at his thin gold wristwatch. 'They'll be here with him in a minute.' He drummed his fingertips on his briefcase. 'If they keep to their schedule.'

'They'll be on time,' Rogers said. 'That's the way they are. They held him four months, but now they'll be on time to prove their good faith all along.' He looked out through the windscreen, past the silent driver's shoulders, at the gateway. The Soviet border guards on the other side – Slavs and stumpy Asiatics in shapeless quilted jackets – were ignoring the Allied

5

squad. They were clustered around a fire in an oil drum in front of their checkpoint shack, holding their hands out to the warmth. Their shroud-barrelled sub-machine-guns were slung over their shoulders, hanging clumsily and unhandily. They were talking and joking, and none of them were bothering to watch the frontier.

'Look at them,' the Foreign Ministry man said peevishly. 'They don't care what we do. They're not concerned if we drive up with an armed squad.'

The Foreign Ministry man was from Geneva, five hundred kilometres away. Rogers had been here, in this sector, for seven years. He shrugged. 'We're all old acquaintances by now. This frontier's been here forty years. They know we're not going to start shooting, any more than they are. This isn't where the war is.'

He looked at the clustered Soviets again, remembering a song he'd heard years ago: 'Give the Comrade With the Machine Gun the Right to Speak.' He wondered if they knew of that song, over on their side of the line. There were many things on the other side of the line that he wanted to know. But there was little hope for it.

The war was in all the world's filing cabinets. The weapon was information: things you knew, things you'd found out about them, things they knew about you. You sent people over the line, or you had them planted from years ago, and you probed. Not many of your people got through. Some of them might. So you put together the little scraps of what you'd found out, hoping it wasn't too garbled, and in the end, if you were clever, you knew what the Soviets were going to do next.

And they probed back. Not many of their people got through – at least, you could be reasonably sure they didn't – but, in the end, they found out what you were going to do next. So neither side did anything. You probed, back and forth, and the deeper you tried to go, the harder it was. For a little distance on either side of the line, there was some light. Further on, there was only a dark fog. And some day, you had to hope, the balance would break in your favour.

The Foreign Ministry man was taking out his impatience in

talk. 'Why the devil did we give Martino a laboratory so near the border in the first place?'

Rogers shook his head. 'I don't know. I don't handle strategy.'

'Well, why couldn't we get a rescue team of our own in there after the explosion?'

'We did. Theirs just got in first. They moved fast and took him away.' And he wondered if that had been a simple piece of luck.

'Why couldn't we take him back from them?'

'I don't handle tactics on that level. I imagine we might have had trouble, though, kidnapping a seriously hurt man out of hospital.' And the man was an American national. Suppose he'd died? The Soviet propaganda teams would have gone to work on the Americans, and when the next A.N.G. bill came up in their Congress, they might not be so quick with their share of next year's budget. Rogers grunted to himself. It was that kind of war.

'I think it's a ridiculous situation. An important man like Martino in their hands, and we're helpless. It's absurd.'

'That's the kind of thing that gives you your work to do, isn't it?'

The Foreign Ministry representative changed his tack. 'I wonder how he's taking it? He was rather badly knocked about in the explosion, I understand.'

'Well, he's convalescent now.'

'I'm told he lost an arm. But I imagine they'll have taken care of that. They're quite good at prosthetics, you know. Why, as far back as the nineteen forties, they were keeping dogs' heads alive with mechanical hearts and so forth.'

'Mm.' A man disappears over the line, Rogers was thinking, and you send out people to find him. Little by little, the reports come trickling in. He's dead, they say. He's lost an arm, but he's alive. He's dying. We don't know where he is. He's been shipped to Novoya Moskva. He's right here, in this city, in a hospital. At least, they've got *somebody* in a hospital here. What hospital?

Nobody knows. You're not going to find out any more. You give what you have to the Foreign Ministry, and the negotiations start. Your side closes down a highway across the line. Their side almost shoots down a plane. Your side impounds some fishing boats. And finally, not so much because of anything your side had done but for some reason of their own, their side gives in.

And all this time, a man from your side has been lying in one of their hospitals, broken and hurt, waiting for you to do something.

'There's a rumour he was quite close to completing something called a K-Eighty-eight,' the Foreign Ministry man went on. 'We had orders not to press too hard, for fear they'd realize how important he was. That is, in the event they didn't already know. But, of course, we were to get him back, so we couldn't go too soft. Delicate business.'

'I can imagine.'

'Do you think they got the K-Eighty-eight out of him?'

'They have a man on their side called Azarin. He's very good.' How can I possibly know until I've talked to Martino? But Azarin's damned good. And I wonder if we shouldn't run this gossip through another security check?

Out beyond the gateway, two headlights bloomed up, turned sideways, and stopped. The rear door of a Tatra limousine snapped open, and at the same time one of the Soviet guards went over to the gate and flipped the rail up. The Allied M.P. sergeant called his men to attention.

Rogers and the Foreign Ministry representative got out of their car.

A man stepped out of the Tatra and came to the gateway. He hesitated at the border and then walked forward quickly between the two rows of M.P.s

'Good God!' the Foreign Ministry man whispered.

The lights glittered in a spray of bluish reflection from the man in the gateway. He was mostly metal.

2

He was wearing one of their shapeless drab civilian suits, with lumpy shoes and a striped brown shirt. His sleeves were too short, and his hands hung far out. One was flesh and one was not. His skull was a polished metal ovoid, completely featureless except for a grille where his mouth ought to be and a half-moon recess, curving upwards at the ends, where his eyes lurked. He stood, looking ill at ease, at the end of two rows of soldiers. Rogers came up to him, holding out his hand. 'Lucas Martino?'

The man nodded. 'Yes.' It was his right hand that was still good. He reached up and took Rogers' hand. His grip was strong and anxious. 'I'm very glad to be here.'

'My name's Rogers. This is Mr Haller, of the Foreign Ministry'

Haller shook Martino's hand automatically, staring.

'How do you do?' Martino said.

'Very well, thank you,' the Foreign Ministry man mumbled. 'And you?'

'The car's over here, Mr Martino,' Rogers cut in. 'I'm with the sector Security office. I'd appreciate it if you came with me. The sooner I interview you, the sooner this'll be completely over.' Rogers touched Martino's shoulder and urged him lightly towards the sedan.

'Yes, of course. There's no need delaying.' The man matched Rogers' quick pace and slipped in ahead of him at his gesture. Haller climbed in on the other side of Martino, and then the driver wheeled the car around and started them rolling for Rogers' office. Behind them, the M.P.s got into their jeeps and followed. Rogers looked back through the car's rear window. The Soviet border guards were staring after them.

Martino sat stiffly against the upholstery, his hands in his lap. 'It feels wonderful to be back,' he said in a strained voice.

'I should think so,' Haller said. 'After what they – '

'I think Mr Martino's only saying what he feels is expected of people in these situations, Mr Haller. I doubt very much if he feels wonderful about anything.'

Haller looked at Rogers with a certain shock. 'You're quite blunt, Mr Rogers.'

'I feel blunt.'

Martino looked from one to the other. 'Please don't let me unsettle you,' he said. 'I'm sorry to be a source of upset. Perhaps it would help if I said I knew what I looked like, and that I, for one, am used to it.'

'Sorry,' Rogers said. 'I didn't mean to start a squabble around you.'

'Please accept my apologies, as well,' Haller added. 'I realize that, in my own way, I was being just as rude as Mr Rogers.'

Martino said, 'And so now we've all apologized to each other.'

So we have, Rogers thought. Everybody's sorry.

They pulled into the ramp which served the side door of Rogers' office building, and the driver stopped the car. 'All right, Mr Martino, this is where we get out,' Rogers told the man. 'Haller, you'll be checking into your office right away?'

'Immediately, Mr Rogers.'

'O.K. I guess your boss and my boss can start getting together on policy towards this.'

'I'm quite sure my Ministry's role in this case was concluded with Mr Martino's safe return,' Haller said delicately. 'I intend to go to bed after I make my report. Good night, Rogers. Pleasure working with you.'

'Of course.' They shook hands briefly, and Rogers followed Martino out of the car and through the side door.

'He washed his hands of me rather quickly, didn't he?' Martino commented as Rogers directed him down a flight of steps into the basement.

Rogers grunted. 'Through this door, please, Mr Martino.'

They came out into a narrow, door-lined corridor with painted concrete walls and a grey linoleum tile floor. Rogers stopped and looked at the doors for a moment. 'That one'll do, I guess. Please come in here with me, Mr Martino.' He took a bunch of keys out of his pocket and unlocked the door.

The room inside was small. It had a cot pushed against one wall, neatly made up with a white pillow and a tightly stretched army blanket. There was a small table, and one chair. An overhead bulb lit the room, and in a side wall there were two doors, one leading to a small closet and the other opening on a compact bathroom.

Martino looked around. 'Is this where you always conduct your interviews with returnees?' he asked mildly.

Rogers shook his head. 'I'm afraid not. I'll have to ask you to stay here for the time being.' He stepped out of the room without giving Martino an opportunity to react. He closed and locked the door.

He relaxed a little. He leaned against the door's solid metal and lit a cigarette with only a faint tremor in his fingertips. Then he walked quickly down the corridor to the automatic elevator and up to the floor where his office was. As he snapped on the lights, his mouth twisted at the thought of what his staff would say when he started calling them out of their beds.

He picked up the telephone on his desk. But first, he had to talk to Deptford, the District Chief. He dialled the number.

Deptford answered almost immediately. 'Hello?' Rogers had expected him to be awake.

'Rogers, Mr Deptford.'

'Hello, Shawn. I've been waiting for your call. Everything go all right with Martino?'

'No, sir. I need an emergency team down here as fast as possible. I want a whatdyoucallit – a man who knows about miniature mechanical devices – with as many assistants authorized as he needs. I want a surveillance device expert. And a psychologist. With the same additional staff authorization for the last two. I want the three key men tonight or tomorrow morning. How much of a staff they'll need'll be up to them, but I want the authorizations in so there won't be any red tape to hold them up. I wish to hell nobody had ever thought of pumping key personnel full of truth-drug allergens.'

'Rogers, what is this? What went wrong? Your offices aren't equipped for any such project as that.'

'I'm sorry, sir. I don't dare move him. There's too many sensitive places in this city. I got him over here and into a cell, and I made damned sure he didn't even get near my office. God knows what he might be after, or can do.'

'Rogers – did Martino come over the line tonight or didn't he?'

Rogers hesitated. 'I don't know,' he said.

3

Rogers ignored the room full of waiting men and sat looking down at the two dossiers, not so much thinking as gathering his energy.

Both dossiers were open at the first page. One was thick, full of security check breakdowns, reports, career progress résumés, and all the other data that accumulate around a government employee through the years. It was labelled *Martino, Lucas Anthony*. The first page was made up of the usual identification statistics: height, weight, colour of eyes, colour of hair, date of birth, fingerprints, dental chart, distinguishing marks and scars. There was a set of standard nude photographs; front, back, and both profiles of a heavy-set, muscular man with controlled, pleasantly intelligent features and a slightly thickened nose.

The second dossier was much thinner. As yet, there was nothing in the folder but the photographs, and it was unlabelled beyond a note: See *Martino, L.A.* (?) The photographs showed a heavy-set, muscular man with broad scars running diagonally up from his left side, across his chest and around his back and both shoulders, like a ropy shawl. His left arm was mechanical up to the top of the shoulder, and seemed to have been grafted directly into his pectoral and dorsal musculature. He had thick scars around the base of his throat, and that metal head.

Rogers stood up behind his desk and looked at the waiting special team. 'Well?'

Barrister, the English servomechanisms engineer, took the bit of his pipe out of his teeth. 'I don't know. It's quite hard to tell on the basis of a few hours' tests.' He took a deep breath. 'As a matter of exact fact, I'm running tests but I've no idea what they'll show, if anything, or how soon.' He gestured helplessly. 'There's no getting *at* someone in his condition. There's no penetrating his surface, as it were. Half our instruments're worthless. There're so many electrical components in his mechanical parts that any readings we take are hopelessly blurred. We can't even do so simple a thing as determine the amperage they used. It hurts him to have us try.' He dropped his voice apologetically. 'It makes him scream.'

Rogers grimaced. 'But he *is* Martino?'

Barrister shrugged.

Rogers suddenly slammed his fist against the top of his desk. 'What the hell are we going to do?'

'Get a can opener,' Barrister suggested.

In the silence, Finchley, who was on loan to Rogers from the American Federal Bureau of Investigation, said, 'Look at this.'

He touched a switch and the film projector he'd brought began to hum while he went over and dimmed the office lights. He pointed the projector towards a blank wall and started the film running. 'Overhead pickup,' he explained. 'Infra-red lighting. We believe he can't see it. We think he was asleep.'

Martino – Rogers had to think of him by that name against his better judgement was lying on his cot. The upturned crescent in his face was shuttered from the inside, with only the edges of a flexible gasket to mark its outline. Below it, the grille, centred just above the blunt curve of his jaw, was ajar. The impression created was vaguely that of a hairless man with his eyes shut, breathing through his mouth. Rogers had to remind himself that this man did not breath.

'This was taken about two a.m. today,' Finchley said. 'He'd been lying there for a little over an hour and a half.'

Rogers frowned at the tinge of bafflement in Finchley's voice. Yes, it was uncanny not being able to tell whether a man was asleep or not. But it was no use doing anything if they were all going to let their nerves go ragged. He almost said something about it until he realized his chest was aching. He relaxed his shoulders, shaking his head at himself.

A cue spot flickered on the film. 'All right,' Finchley said, 'now listen.' The tiny speaker in the projector began to crackle.

Martino had begun to thrash on his cot, his metal arm striking sparks from the wall.

Rogers winced.

Abruptly, the man started to babble in his sleep. The words poured out, each syllable distinct. But the speech was wildly faster than normal, and the voice was desperate:

'Name! Name! Name!

'Name Lucas Martino born Bridgetown New Jersey May tenth nineteen forty-eight, about . . . *face*! Detail . . . *for*ward . . . *march*!

'Name! Name! Detail . . . Halt!

'Name Lucas Martino born Bridgetown New Jersey May tenth nineteen forty-eight!'

Rogers felt Finchley touch his arm. 'Think they were walking him?'

Rogers shrugged. 'If that's a genuine nightmare, and if that's Martino, then, yes – it sounds very much like they were walking him back and forth in a small room and firing questions at him. You know their technique: keep a man on his feet, keep him moving, keep asking questions. Change interrogation teams every few hours, so they'll be fresh. Don't let the subject sleep or get off his feet. Walk him delirious. Yes, that's what it might be.'

'Do you think he's faking?'

'I don't know. He may have been. Then again, maybe he was asleep. Maybe he's one of their people, and he was dreaming we were trying to shake his story.'

After a time, the man on the cot fell back. He lay still, his forearms raised stiffly from the elbows, his hands curled into rigid claws. He seemed to be looking straight up at the camera with his streamlined face, and no one could tell whether he was awake or asleep, thinking or not, afraid or in pain, or who or what he was.

Finchley shut off the projector.

4

Rogers had been awake for thirty-six hours. It was a whole day, now, since the man had come back over the line. Rogers pawed angrily at his burning eyes as he let himself into his apartment. He left his clothes in a rumpled trail across the threadbare old carpet as he crossed the floor towards the bathroom. Fumbling in the medicine cabinet for an Alka-Seltzer, he envied the little wiry men like Finchley who could stay awake for days without their stomachs backing up on them.

The clanking pipes slowly filled the tub with hot brown water while he pulled at his beard with a razor. He clawed his fingers through the crisp, cropped red hair on his scalp, and scowled at the dandruff that came flaking out.

God, he thought wearily, I'm thirty-seven and I'm coming apart.

As he slid into the tub, feeling the hot water working into

the bad hip where he'd been hit by a cobblestone in a riot, looking down under his navel at the bulge that no exercise could quite flatten out any more, the thought drove home.

A few more years, and I'll really have a pot. When the damp weather comes, that hip's going to give me all kinds of hell. I used to be able to stay up two or three days at a clip – I'm never going to be able to do that again. Some day I'm going to try some stunt I could do the week before, and I won't make it.

Some day, too, I'm going to make a decision of some kind – some complex, either – or thing that's got to be right. I'll know I've got it right – and it'll be wrong. I'll start screwing up, and every time after that I'll get the inside sweats remembering how I was wrong. I'll start pressing, and worrying, and living on dexedrine, and if they spot it in time, upstairs, they'll give me a nice harmless job in a corner somewhere. And if they don't spot it, one of these days Azarin's going to put a really good one over on me, and everybody's kids'll talk Chinese.

He shivered. The phone rang in the living-room.

He climbed out of the tub, holding carefully on to the edge, and wrapped himself in one of the huge towels that was the size of a blanket, and which he was going to take back to the States with him if he was ever assigned there. He padded out to the phone stand and picked up the head-piece. 'Yeah?'

'Mr Rogers?' He recognized one of the War Ministry operators.

'That's right.'

'Mr Deptford is on the line. Hold on, please.'

'Thank you.' He waited, wishing the cigarette box wasn't across the room beside his bed.

'Shawn? Your office said you'd be home.'

'Yes, sir. My shirt was trying to walk off me.'

'I'm here, at the Ministry. I've just been talking to the Under-secretary for Security. How are you doing on this Martino business? Have you reached any definite conclusions yet?'

Rogers thought over the terms of his answer. 'No, sir, I'm sorry. We've only had one day, so far.'

'Yes, I know. Do you have any notion of how much more time you'll need?'

Rogers frowned. He had to calculate how much time they could possibly spare. 'I'd say a week.' He hoped.

'That long?'

'I'm afraid so. The team's set up and working smoothly now, but we're having a very rough time. He's like a big egg.'

'I see.' Deptford took a long breath that came clearly over the phone. 'Shawn – Karl Schwenn asked me if you knew how important Martino is to us.'

Rogers said quietly: 'You can tell Mr Under-secretary I know my job.'

'All right, Shawn. He wasn't trying to rag you. He just wanted to be certain.'

'What you mean is, he's riding you.'

Deptford hesitated. 'Someone's riding him, too, you know.'

'I could still stand to do with a little less Teutonic discipline in this department.'

'Have you been to sleep lately, Shawn?'

'No, sir. I'll be filing daily reports, and when we crack this, I'll phone.'

'Very well, Shawn. I'll tell him. Good night.'

'Good night, sir.'

He hung up and the red scrambler bulb on the phone went out. He went back into the bathtub and lay there with his eyes closed, letting Martino's dossier drift up into the forepart of his brain.

There was still very little in it. The man was still five feet eleven inches tall. His weight was up to two hundred and sixty-eight pounds. His arches had collapsed, but the thickness of his skull plating apparently made up the height differential.

Nothing else in the I.D. chart was applicable. There were no entries for eyes, hair, or complexion. There was no entry for Date of Birth, though a physiologist had given him an age, within the usual limits of error, that corresponded with 1948. Fingerprints? Distinguishing marks and scars?

Rogers' bitter smile was pale at the corners. He dried himself, kicked his old clothes into a corner, and dressed. He went back into the bathroom, dropped his toothbrush into his pocket, thought for a moment and added the tube of Alka-Seltzer, and went back to his office.

It was early in the morning of the second day. Rogers looked across his desk at Willis, the psychologist.

'If they were going to let Martino go anyway,' Rogers asked, 'why would they go to so much trouble with him? He wouldn't have needed all that hardware just to keep him alive. Why did they carefully make an exhibition piece out of him?'

Willis rubbed a hand over the stubble on his face. 'Assuming he's Martino, they may never have intended to let him go. I agree with you – if they were going to give him back to us originally, they'd probably just have patched him up any old way. Instead, they went to a great deal of trouble to rebuild him as close to a functioning human being as possible.

'I think what happened was that they knew he'd be useful to them. They expected a great deal from him, and they wanted him to be as physically capable of delivering it as they could make him. It's quite probable they never even considered how he'd look to us. Oh, they may have gone beyond the absolute necessary minimum in dressing him up – but perhaps it was him they wanted to impress. In any case, they probably thought he'd be grateful to them, and that might give them a wedge. And let's not discount this idea of arousing his purely professional admiration. Particularly since he's a physicist. That could be quite a bridge between him and their culture. If that was one of the considerations, I'd say it was excellent psychological technique.'

Rogers lit a new cigarette, grimacing at the taste. 'We've been over this before. We can play with almost any notion we want to and make it fit some of the few facts we know. What does it prove?'

'Well, as I said, they may never have intended to let us see him again. If we work with that as an assumption, then why did they finally let him go? Aside from the pressure we exerted on them, let's say he held out. Let's say they finally saw he wasn't going to be the gold mine they'd expected. Let's say they've got something else planned – next month, say, or next week. Looking at it that way, it's reasonable for them to have let him go, figuring also that if they give Martino back, maybe they can get away with their next stunt.'

'That's too many assumptions. What's he got to say on the subject?'

Willis shrugged. 'He says they made him some offers. He decided they were just bait and turned them down. He says they interrogated him and he didn't crack.'

'Think it's possible?'

'Anything's possible. He hasn't gone insane yet. That's something in itself. He was always a pretty firmly balanced individual.'

Rogers snorted. 'Look – they cracked everybody they ever wanted to crack. Why not him?'

'I'm not saying they didn't. But there's a possibility he's telling the truth. Maybe they didn't have enough time. Maybe he had an advantage over their usual subjects. Not having mobile features and a convulsed respiratory cycle to show when they had him close to the ragged edge – that might be a big help.'

'Yes,' Rogers said. 'I'm becoming aware of that possibility.'

'His heartbeat's no indicator, either, with a good part of the load taken over by his powerplant. I'm told his entire metabolic cycle's non-kosher.'

'I can't figure it,' Rogers said. 'I can't figure it at all. Either he's Martino or he isn't. They went to all this trouble. Now we've got him back. If he's Martino, I still don't see what they hope to gain. I can't accept the notion they don't hope to gain anything – that's not like them.'

'Not like us, either.'

'All right. Look – we're two sides, each convinced we're right and the other fellow's wrong. This century's thrashing out the world's way of life for the next thousand years. When you're playing for stakes like that, you don't miss a step. If he isn't Martino, they might have known we wouldn't just take him back without checking him. If this's their idea of a smart trick for slipping us a ringer, they're dumber than their past performance chart reads. But if he *is* Martino, why did they let him go? Did he go over to them? God knows, whole countries went Soviet that we never thought would.'

He rubbed the top of his head. 'They've got us chasing our tails over this guy.'

Willis nodded sourly. 'I know. Listen – how much do you know about the Russians?'

'Russians? About as much as I do about the other Soviets. Why?'

Willis said reluctantly. 'Well, it's a trap to generalize about these things. But there's something we had to learn to take into account, down at PsychoWar. It's a Slav's idea of a joke. Particularly the Russians'. I keep thinking . . whether it started out that way or not, every one of them that knows about this fellow is laughing at us now. They go in for deadpan practical jokes, and especially the kind where somebody bleeds a little. I've got a vision of the boys in Novoya Moska clustered around the vodka at night and laughing and laughing and laughing.'

'That's nice,' Rogers said. 'That's very fine.' He wiped his palm over his jaw. 'That helps.'

'I thought you'd enjoy it.'

'God damn it, Willis, I've *got* to crack that shell of his! We can't have him running around loose and unsolved. Martino was one of the very best in his business. He was right up there, right in the thick of every new wrinkle we're going to pleat for the next ten years. He was working on this K-Eighty-eight thing. And the Soviets had him for four months. What'd they get out of him, what'd they do to him – do they still have him?'

'I know . . .' Willis said slowly. 'I can see he might have given away almost anything, or even become an active agent of theirs. But on this business of his not being Martino at all – I frankly can't believe that. What about the fingerprints on his one good hand?'

Rogers cursed. 'His right shoulder's a mass of scar tissue. If they can substitute mechanical parts for eyes and ears and lungs – if they can motorize an arm and graft it right into him – where does that leave us?'

Willis turned pale. 'You mean – they could fake anything. It's definitely Martino's right arm, but it isn't necessarily Martino.'

'That's right.'

The telephone rang. Rogers rolled over on his cot and lifted the receiver off the unit on the floor beside him. 'Rogers,' he mumbled. 'Yes, Mr Deptford.' The radiant numerals on his watch were swimming before his eyes, and he blinked sharply to steady them. Eleven-thirty p.m. He'd been asleep a little under two hours.

'Hello, Shawn. I've got your third daily report in front of me here. I'm sorry to have awakened you, but you don't really seem to be making much progress, do you?'

'That's all right. About waking me up, I mean. No – no, I'm not getting far on this thing.'

The office was dark except for the seep of light under the door from the hall. Across the hall, in a larger office Rogers had commandeered, a specialist clerical staff was collating and evaluating the reports Finchley, Barrister, Willis, and the rest of them had made. Rogers could faintly hear the restless clacking of typewriters and I.B.M. machines.

'Would it be of any value for me to come down?'

'And take over the investigation? Come ahead. Any time.'

Deptford said nothing for a moment. Then he asked, 'Would I get any further than you have?'

'No.'

'That's what I told Karl Schwenn.'

'Still giving you the business, is he?'

'Shawn, he has to. The entire K-Eighty-eight programme has been held up for months. No other project in the world would have been permitted to hang fire this long. At the first doubt of its security, it would have been washed out as a matter of routine. You know that, and that ought to tell you how important the K-Eighty-eight is. I think you're aware of what's going on in Africa at this moment. We've got to have something to show. We've got to quiet the Soviets down – at least until they've developed something to match it. The Ministry's putting pressure on this Department to reach a quick decision on this man.'

'I'm sorry, sir. We're almost literally taking this man apart like a bomb. But we don't have anything to show whose bomb he is.'

'There must be something.'

'Mr Deptford, when we send a man over the line, we provide him with their I.D. papers. We go further. We fill his pockets with their coins, their door keys, their cigarettes, their combs. We give him one of their billfolds, with their sales receipts and laundry tickets. We give him photographs of relatives and girls, printed on their kind of paper with their processes and chemicals – and yet every one of those items came out of our manufacturing shops and never saw the other side of the line before.'

Deptford sighed. 'I know. How's he taking it?'

'I can't tell. When one of our people goes over the line, he has a cover story. He's an auto mechanic, or a baker, or a tramway conductor. And if he's one of our good people – and for important jobs we only send the best – then, no matter what happens, no matter what they do to him – he *stays* a baker or a tramway conductor. He answers questions like a tramway conductor. He's as bewildered at it all as a tramway conductor would be. If necessary, he bleeds and screams and dies like a tramway conductor.'

'Yes.' Deptford's voice was quiet. 'Yes, he does. Do you suppose Azarin ever wonders if perhaps this man he's working on really *is* a tramway conductor?'

'Maybe he does, sir. But he can't ever act as if he did, or he wouldn't be doing his job.'

'All right, Shawn. But we've got to have our answer soon.'

'I know.'

After a time, Deptford said: 'It's been pretty rough on you, hasn't it, Shawn?'

'Some.'

'You've always done the job for me.' Deptford's voice was quiet, and then Rogers heard the peculiar click a man's drying lips make as he opens his mouth to wet them. 'All right. I'll explain the situation upstairs, and you do what you can.'

'Yes, sir. Thank you.'

'Good night, Shawn. Go back to sleep, if you can.'

'Good night, sir.' Rogers hung up. He sat looking down at the darkness around his feet. It's funny, he thought. I wanted an education, and my family lived half a block away from the docks at Brooklyn. I wanted to be able to understand what a categorical imperative was, and recognize a quote from Byron when I heard one. I wanted to wear a tweed jacket and smoke a pipe under a campus oak somewhere. And during the summers while I was going to high school, I worked for this insurance company, file clerking in the claims investigation division. So when I got the chance to try for that A.N.G. scholarship, I took it. And when they found out I knew something about investigation work, they put me in with their Security trainees. And here I am, and I never thought about it one way or another. I've got a pretty good record. Pretty damned good. But I wonder, now, if I wouldn't have done just as well at something else?

Then he slowly put his shoes on, went to his desk, and clicked on the light.

7

The week was almost over. They were beginning to learn things, but none of them were the slightest help.

Barrister laid the first engineering drawing down on Rogers' desk. 'This is how his head works – we believe. It's a difficult thing, not being able to get clear X-rays.'

Rogers looked down at the drawing and grunted. Barrister began pointing out specific details, using his pipestem to tap the drawing.

'There's his eye assembly. He has binocular vision, with servo-motored focusing and tracking. The motors are powered by this miniature pile, in his chest cavity, here. So are the remainder of his artificial components. It's interesting to note he's a complete selection of filters for his eye lenses. They did him up brown. By the by, he *can* see by infra-red if he wants to.'

Rogers spat a shred of tobacco off his lower lip. 'That's interesting.'

Barrister said, 'Now – right here, on each side of the eyes, are two acoustical pickups. Those are his ears. They must have felt it was better design to house both functions in that one central skull opening. It's directional, but not as effective as God intended. Here's something else; the shutter that closes that opening is quite tough – armoured to protect all those delicate components. The result is he's deaf when his eyes're closed. He probably sleeps more restfully for it.'

'When he isn't faking nightmares, yeah.'

'Or having them.' Barrister shrugged. 'Not my department.'

'I wish it wasn't mine. All right, now what about that other hole?'

'His mouth? Well, there's a false, immovable jaw over the working one – again, apparently, to protect the mechanism. His true jaws, his saliva ducts, and teeth are artificial. His tongue isn't. The inside of the mouth is plastic-lined. Teflon, probably, or one of its kin. My people're having a little trouble breaking it down for analysis. But he's cooperative about letting us gouge out samples.'

Rogers licked his lips. 'Okay – fine,' he said brusquely. 'But how's all this hooked into his brain? How does he operate it?'

Barrister shook his head. 'I don't know. He used it all as if he were born with it, so there's some sort of connexion into his voluntary and autonomic nervous centres. But we don't yet know exactly how it was done. He's cooperative, as I said, but I'm not the man to start disassembling any of this – we might not be able to put him back together again. All I know is that somewhere, behind all that machinery, there's a functioning human brain inside that skull. How the Soviets did it is something else again. You have to remember they've been fiddling with this sort of thing a long time.' He laid another sheet atop the first one, paying no attention to the pallor of Rogers' face.

'Here's his powerplant. It's only roughed out in the drawing, but we think it's just a fairly ordinary pocket pile. It's located where his lungs were, next to the blower that operates his vocal chords and the most ingenious oxygen circulator I've ever heard of. The delivered power's electrical, of course, and it works his arm, his jaws, his audiovisual equipment, and everything else.'

'How well's the pile shielded?'

Barrister let a measured amount of professional admiration show in his voice. 'Well enough so we can get muddy X-rays right around it. There's *some* leakage, of course. He'll die in about fifteen years.'

'Mm.'

'Well, now, man, if they cared whether he lived or died, they'd have supplied us with blueprints.'

'They cared at one time. And fifteen years might be plenty long enough for them, if he isn't Martino.'

'And if he is Martino?'

'Then, if he is Martino, and they got to him with some of their persuasions, fifteen years might be plenty long enough for them.'

'And if he's Martino and they didn't get to him? If he's the same man he always was, behind his new armour? If he isn't the Man from Mars? If he's simply plain Lucas Martino, physicist?'

Rogers shook his head slowly. 'I don't know. I'm running out of ideas for quick answers. But we have to find out. Before we're through, we may have to find out everything he ever did or felt – everyone he talked to, everything he thought.'

Chapter 2

Lucas Martino was born in the hospital of the large town nearest to his father's farm. His mother was injured by the birth, and so he was both the eldest son and only child of Matteo and Serafina Martino, truck farmers, of Milano, near Bridgetown, New Jersey. He was named after the uncle who had paid his parents' passage to the United States in 1947 and lent them the money for the farm.

Milano, New Jersey, was a community of tomato fields, peach orchards, and chicken farms, centring on a general store which sold household staples, stock feed, petrol for the tractors, and was also the post office. One mile to the north, the four broad lanes of a concrete highway carried booming traffic between Camden-Philadelphia and Atlantic City. To the west, railroad tracks curved down from Camden to Cape May. To the south, forming the base of a triangle of communications, another highway ran from the Jersey shore to the Chester ferry across the mouth of the Delaware, and so connected to all the sprawling highways of the Eastern Seaboard. Bridgetown lay at the meeting of railroad and highway, but Milano was inside the triangle, never more than five minutes away from the world as most people knew it, and yet far enough.

Half a century earlier, the clayey earth had been planted with acre-on-acre of vineyard, and the Malaga Processing Corporation had imported workers by the hundreds from old Italy. Communities had grown up, farms had been cleared, and the language of the area was Italian.

When the grape blight came, the tight cultural pattern was torn. Some, like Lucas Maggiore, left the farms their fathers had built and moved to the Italian communities in other cities. To a certain extent their places were taken by people from

25

different parts of the world. And the newcomers, too, were all farmers by birth and blood. In a few years the small communities were once again reasonably prosperous, set in a new pattern of habits and customs that was much like the old. But the outside world had touched the little towns like Milano, and in turn Milano had sent out some of its own people to the world as most of us know it.

The country was warm in the summer, with mild winters. The outlying farms were set among patches of pine and underbrush, and there were wide-eyed deer that came into the kitchen gardens during the winter. Most of the roads were graded gravel, and the utility poles carried only one or two strands of cable. There were more pickup trucks than cars on the roads, though the cars were as likely to be new Dodges and Mercurys as not. There was a tomato-packing plant a few miles up the road, and Matteo Martino's farm was devoted mostly to tomato vines. Except for occasional trips to Bridgetown for dress material and parts for the truck, the packing plant and general store were as far from home as Matteo ever found it necessary to go.

Young Lucas had heavy bones and an already powerful frame from Matteo's North Italian ancestry. His eyes were brown, but his hair at that age was almost light enough to be blond. His father had a habit of occasionally rumpling his hair and calling him Tedeschino – which means 'the little German' – to his mother's faint annoyance. They lived together in a four-roomed farmhouse, a closely knit unit, and Lucas grew naturally into a share of the work. They were three people with three different but interdependent responsibilities, as they had to be if the work was to go properly. Serafina kept house and helped with the picking. Matteo did the heavy work, and Lucas, more and more as he grew older and stronger, did the necessary maintenance work that had to be kept up day by day. He weeded, he had charge of racking and storing the hand tools, and Matteo, who had worked in the Fiat plant before he came to America, was gradually teaching him how to repair and maintain the tractor. Lucas had a bent for mechanics.

Having no brothers or sisters, and being too busy to talk much with his parents during the day, he grew into early adolescence alone, but not lonely. For one thing, he had more than the ordinary share of work to keep him occupied. For another, he thought in terms of shaped parts that fitted into other parts to produce a whole, functioning mechanism. Having no one near his own age whose growth and development he could observe, he learned to observe himself – to stand a little to one side of the young boy and catalogue the things he did, putting each new discovery into its proper place in an already well-disciplined and instinctively systematic brain. From the outside, no doubt, he seemed to be an overly serious, preoccupied youngster.

Through grammar school, which he attended near his home, he formed no important outside associations. He returned home for lunch and immediately after school, because there was always work to do and because he wanted to. He got high marks in all subjects but English, which he spoke fluently but not often enough or long enough to become interested in its grammatic structure. However, he did well enough at it, and when he was thirteen he was enrolled in the high school at Bridgetown, twelve road miles away by bus.

Twenty-four miles by bus, every day, in the company of twenty other people your own age – people named Morgan, Crosby, Muller, Kovacs, and Jones in addition to those named Del Bello and Scarpa – can do things. In particular, they can do things to a quiet, self-sufficient young boy with constantly inquiring eyes. His trouble with grammar disappeared overnight. Morgan taught him to smoke. Kovacs talked about the structure of music, and with Del Bello he went out for football. Most important, in his sophomore year he met Edmund Starke, a short, thickset, reticent man with rimless glasses who taught the physics class. It would take a little time, a little study, and a little growth. But Lucas Martino was on his way out into the world.

Chapter 3

It was a week after the man had come across the line. Dept-ford's voice was tired and empty over the phone. Rogers, whose ears had been buzzing faintly but constantly during the past two days, had to jam the headpiece hard against his ear in order to make out what he was saying.

'I showed Karl Schwenn all your reports, Shawn, and I added a summary of my own. He agrees that nothing more could have been done.'

'Yes, sir.'

'He was a sector chief himself once, you know. He's aware of these things.'

'Yes, sir.'

'In a sense, this sort of thing happens to us every day. If anything, it happens to the Soviets even more often. I like to think we take longer to reach these decisions than they do.'

'I suppose so.'

Deptford's voice was oddly inconclusive in tone, now, as though he were searching his mind for something to say that would round things off. But it was a conversation born to trail away rather than end, and Deptford gave up after only a short pause.

'That's it, then. Tomorrow you can disperse the team, and you're to stand by until you're notified what policy we're going to pursue with regard to Mar – to the man.'

'All right, sir.'

'Good-bye, Shawn.'

'Good night, Mr Deptford.' He put the receiver down and rubbed his ear.

Rogers and Finchley sat on the edge of the cot and looked across the tiny room at the faceless man, who was sitting in the one chair beside the small table on which he ate his meals. He had been kept in this room through most of the week, and had gone out of it only to the laboratory rigged in the next room. He had been given new clothes. He had used the bathroom shower several times without rusting.

'Now, Mr Martino,' the F.B.I. man was saying politely. 'I know we've asked before, but have you remembered anything new since our last talk?'

One last try, Rogers thought. You always give it one whack for luck before you give up.

He hadn't yet told anyone on the team that they were all through. He'd asked Finchley to come down here with him because it was always better to have more than one man in on an interrogation. If the subject started to weaken, you could ask questions alternatively, bouncing him back and forth between you like a tennis ball, and his head would swing from one man to the other as though he were watching himself in flight.

No – no, Rogers thought, to hell with that. I just didn't want to come down here alone.

The overhead light winked on polished metal. It was only after a second or two that Rogers realized the man had shaken his head in answer to Finchley's question.

'No, I don't remember a thing. I can remember being caught in the blast – it looked like it was coming straight at my face.' He barked a savage, throaty laugh. 'I guess it was. I woke up in their hospital and put my one hand up to my head.' His right arm went up to his hard cheek as though to help him remember. It jerked back down abruptly, almost in shock, as if that were exactly what had happened the first time.

'Uh-huh,' Finchley said quickly. 'Then what?'

'That night they shot a needle full of some anaesthetic into my spine. When I woke up again, I had this arm.'

The motorized limb flashed up and his knuckles rang faintly against his skull. Either from the conducted sound or the memory of that first astonished moment, Martino winced visibly.

His face fascinated Rogers. The two lenses of his eyes, collecting light from all over the room, glinted darkly in their recess. The grilled shutter set flush in his mouth opening looked like a row of teeth barred in a desperate grimace.

Of course, behind that façade a man who wasn't Martino might be smiling in thin laughter at the team's efforts to crack past it.

'Lucas,' Rogers said as softly as he could, not looking in the man's direction, fogging the verbal pitch low and inside.

Martino's head turned towards him without a second's hesitation. 'Yes, Mr Rogers?'

Ball One. If he'd been trained, he'd been well trained.

'Did they interrogate you extensively?'

The man nodded. 'I don't know what you'd consider extensive in a case like this of course. But I was up and around after two months; they were able to talk to me for several weeks before that. In all, I'd say they spent about ten weeks trying to get me to tell them something they didn't already know.'

'Something about the K-Eighty-eight, you mean?'

'I didn't mention the K-Eighty-eight. I don't think they know about it. They just asked general questions: what lines of investigation we were pursuing – things like that.'

Ball Two.

'Well, look, Mr Martino,' Finchley said, and Martino's skull moved uncannily on his neck, like a tank's turret swivelling. 'They went to a lot of trouble with you. Frankly, if we'd got to you first there's a chance you might be alive today, yes, but you wouldn't like yourself very much.'

The metal arm twitched sharply against the side of the desk. There was an over-long silence. Rogers half expected some bitter answer from the man.

'Yes, I see what you mean.' Rogers was surprised at the complete detachment in the slightly muffled voice. 'They wouldn't have done it if they hadn't expected some pretty positive return on their investment.'

Finchley looked helplessly at Rogers. Then he shrugged. 'I guess you've said it about as specifically as possible,' he told Martino.

'They didn't get it, Mr Finchley. Maybe because they outdid themselves. It's pretty tough to crack a man who doesn't show his nerves.'

A home run, over the centrefield bleachers and still rising when last seen.

Rogers' calves pushed the cot back with a scrape against the cement floor when he stood up. 'All right, Mr Martino. Thank you. And I'm sorry we haven't been able to reach any conclusion.'

The man nodded. 'So am I.'

Rogers watched him closely. 'There's one more thing. You know one of the reasons we pushed you so hard was because the government was anxious about the future of the K-Eighty-eight programme.'

'Yes?'

Rogers bit his lip. 'I'm afraid that's all over now. They couldn't wait any longer.'

Martino looked quickly from Rogers to Finchley's face, and back again. Rogers could have sworn his eyes glowed with a light of their own. There was a splintering crack and Rogers stared at the edge of the desk where the man's hand had closed on it convulsively.

'I'm not ever going back to work, am I?' the man demanded.

He pushed himself away from the desk and stood as though his remaining muscles, too, had been replaced by steel cables under tension.

Rogers shook his head. 'I couldn't say, officially. But I don't see how they'd dare let a man of your ability get near any critical work. Of course, there's still a policy decision due on your case. So I can't say definitely until it reaches me.'

Martino paced three steps towards the end of the room, spun, and paced back.

Rogers found himself apologizing to the man. 'They couldn't take the risk. They're probably trying some alternate approach to the problem K-Eighty-eight was supposed to handle.'

Martino slapped his thigh.

'Probably that monstrosity of Besser's.' He sat down abruptly, facing away from them. His hand fumbled at his shirt pocket and he pushed the end of a cigarette through his mouth grille. A motor whined, and the split soft rubber inner gasket closed around it. He lit the cigarette with jerky motions of his good arm.

'Damn it,' he muttered savagely. 'Damn it, K-Eighty-eight was *the* answer! They'll go broke trying to make that abortion of Besser's work.' He took an angry drag on the cigarette.

Suddenly he spun his head around and looked squarely at Rogers. 'What in hell are *you* staring at? I've got a throat and a tongue. Why shouldn't I smoke?'

'We know that, Mr Martino,' Finchley said gently.

Martino's red gaze shifted. 'You just think you do.' He turned back to face the wall. 'Weren't you two about to leave?'

Rogers nodded silently before he spoke. 'Yes. Yes, we were, Mr Martino. We'll be going. Sorry.'

'All right.' He sat without speaking until they were almost out of the door. Then he said, 'Can you get me some lens tissue?'

'I'll send some in right away.' Rogers closed the door gently. 'His eyes must get dirty, at that,' he commented to Finchley.

The F.B.I. man nodded absently, walking along the hall beside him.

Rogers said uncomfortably, 'That was quite a show he put on. If he is Martino, I don't blame him.'

Finchley grimaced. 'And if he isn't, I don't blame him either.'

'You know,' Rogers said, 'if we'd been able to crack him today, they would have kept the K-Eighty-eight programme going. It won't actually be scrubbed until midnight. It was more or less up to me.'

'Oh?'

Rogers nodded. 'I told him it was washed out because I wanted to see what he'd do. I suppose I thought he might make some kind of break.'

Rogers felt a peculiar kind of defeat. He had run down. He was empty of energy, and everything from now on would only be a falling downhill, back the way he had come.

'Well,' Finchley said, 'you can't say he didn't react.'

'Yes, he did. He reacted.' Rogers found himself disliking the sound of what he would say. 'But he didn't react in any way that would help. All he did was act like a normal human being.'

Chapter 4

The Physics Laboratory at Bridgetown Memorial High School was a longish room with one wall formed by the windows of the building front. It was furnished with long, varnished, masonite-topped tables running towards the end of the room where Edmund Starke's desk was set on a raised platform. Blackboards ran along two of the remaining walls, and equipment cupboards took up the other. By and large, the room was adequate for its purpose, neither substandard nor good enough to satisfy Starke, neither originally designed to be a laboratory nor rendered hopelessly unsuited by its conversion from two ordinary classrooms. It was intended to serve as the space enclosing the usual high school physics class, and that was what it was.

Lucas Martino saw it as something else again, though he didn't realize it and for quite some time couldn't have said why. But never once did he remind himself that a highly similar class might have been held in any high school in the world. This was *his* physics class, taught by *his* instructor, in *his* laboratory. This was *the* place, in its place, as everything in his universe was in its place or beginning to near it. So when he came in each day he first looked around it searchingly before he took his chair at one of the tables, with an unmistakably contented and oddly proprietary expression. Consequently, Starke marked him out for an eager student.

Lucas Martino couldn't ignore a fact. He judged no fact; he only filed it away, like a machine part found on a workshop bench, confident that some day he would find the part to which it fitted, knowing that some day all these parts would, by inevitable process, join together in a complete mechanism which he would put to use. Furthermore, everything he saw

33

represented a fact to him. He made no judgements, so nothing was trivial. Everything he had ever seen or heard was put somewhere in his brain. His memory was not photographic – he wasn't interested in a static picture of his past – but it was all-inclusive. People said his mind was a jumble of odd knowledge. And he was always trying to fit these things together, and see to what mechanism they led.

In classes, he was quiet and answered only when asked to. He had the habit of depending on himself to fit his own facts together, and the notion of consulting someone else – even Starke – by asking an impromptu question was foreign to him. He was accustomed to a natural order of things in which few answers were supplied. Asking Starke to help him with his grasp of facts would have seemed unfair to him.

Consequently, his marks showed unpredictable ups and downs. Like all high school science classes, the only thing Starke's physics class was supposed to teach was the principal part of the broad theoretical base. His students were given and expected to learn by rote the various simpler laws and formulae, like so many bricks ripped whole out of a misty and possibly useful structure. They were not yet – if ever – expected to construct anything of their own out of them. Lucas Martino failed to realize this. He would have been uncomfortable with the thought. It was his notion that Starke was throwing out hints, and he was presumed capable of filling in the rest for himself.

So there were times when he saw the inevitable direction of a lecture before its first sentences were cold, and when he leaped to the conclusion of an experiment before Starke had the apparatus fairly set up. One thing after another would fall into place for him, garnering its structure out of his storehouse of half-ideas, hints, and unrelated data. When this happened, he'd experienced what someone else would have called a flash of genius.

But there were other times when things only seemed to fit, when actually they did not, and then he shot down a blind alley in pursuit of a hare-brained mistake, making some ridiculous error no one else would have made or could have.

When this happened, he painfully worked his way back

along the false chain of facts, taking each in turn and examining it to see why he'd been fooled, eventually returning to the right track. But, having once built a structure, he found it impossible to discard it entirely. So another part of his mind was a storehouse of interesting ideas that hadn't worked, but were interesting – theories that were wild, but had seemed to hold together. To a certain extent, these phantom heresies stayed behind to colour his thinking. He would never quite be an orthodox theory-spieler.

Meanwhile, he went on gathering facts.

Starke was a veteran of the high school teaching circuit. He'd seen his share of morning glories and of impassive average-mechanics working for the Valedictorian's chair on graduation night. He'd got past the point of resenting them, and long before that he'd got past the point of wasting his conversation on them. He found out early in the game that their interests were not in common with his own.

So Lucas Martino attracted him and he felt obligated to establish some kind of link with the boy. He took several weeks to find the opportunity, and even then he had to force it. He was clumsy, because sociability wasn't his forte. He was an economical man, saw no reason to establish social relations with anyone he didn't respect, and respected few people.

Lucas was finishing up a report at the end of a class when Starke levered himself out of his chair, waited for the rest of the class to start filing out, and walked over to the boy.

'Martino –'

Lucas looked up, surprised but not startled. 'Yes, Mr Starke?'

'Uh – you're not a member of the Physics Club, are you?'

'No, sir.' The Physics Club existed as yet another excuse for a group picture in the yearbook.

'Well – I've been thinking of having the club perform some special experiments. Outside of class. Might even work up some demonstrations and stage them at an assembly. I thought the rest of the student body might be interested.' All of this was sheer fabrication, arrived at on the spur of the moment, and Starke was astonished at himself. 'Wondered if you'd care to join in.'

Lucas shook his head. 'Sorry, Mr Starke. I don't have much extra time, with football practice and work at night.'

Ordinarily, Starke wouldn't have pressed further. Now he said, 'Come on, Martino. Frank Del Bello's on the team, too, and he's a member of the club.'

For some reason, Lucas felt as though Starke were probing an exposed nerve. After all, as far as Lucas Martino knew up to this moment, he had no rational basis for considering the physics class any more important than his other courses. But he reacted sharply and quickly. 'I'm afraid I'm not interested in popular science, Mr Starke.' He immediately passed over the fact that belonging to the club as it was and following Starke's new programme were two different things. He wasn't interested in fine argumentative points. He clearly understood that Starke was after something else entirely, and that Starke, with his momentum gathered, would keep pushing. 'I don't think that demonstrating nuclear fission by dropping a cork into a bunch of mousetraps has anything to do with physics. I'm sorry.'

It was suddenly a ticklish moment for both of them. Starke was unused to being stopped once he'd started something. Lucas Martino lived by facts, and the facts of the circumstances left him only one position to take, as he saw it. In a very real sense, each felt the other's mass resisting him, and each knew that something violent could result unless they found some neutral way to disengage.

'What *is* your idea of physics, Martino?'

Lucas took the opening and turned into it gratefully. He found it led farther than he'd thought. 'I think it's the most important thing in the world, sir,' he said, and felt like a man stumbling out over a threshold.

'You do, eh? Why?' Starke slammed the door behind him.

Lucas fumbled for words. 'The universe is a perfect structure. Everything in it is in balance. It's complete. Nothing can be added to it or taken away.'

'And what does that mean?'

Bit by bit, facts were falling together in Lucas Martino's mind. Ideas, half-thoughts, bits of information that he failed to recognize as fragments of a philosophy – all these things suddenly arranged themselves in a systematic and natural order as he listened to what he'd just said on impulse. For the first time since the day he'd come to this class with a fresh, blank, laboratory notebook, he understood exactly what he was doing here. He understood more than that; he understood himself. His picture of himself was complete, finished for all time.

That left him free to turn to something else.

'Well, Martino?'

Lucas took one deep breath, and stopped fumbling. 'The universe is constructed of perfectly fitted parts. Every time you rearrange the position of one, you affect all the others. If you add something in one place, you had to take it away from somewhere else. Everything we do – everything that has ever been done – was accomplished by rearranging pieces of the universe. If we knew exactly where everything fitted, and what moving it would do to all the other pieces, we'd be able to do things more effectively. That's what physics is doing – investigating the structure of the universe and giving us a system to handle it with. That's the most basic thing there is. Everything else depends on it.'

'That's an article of faith with you, is it?'

'That's the way it *is*. Faith has nothing to do with it.' The answer came quickly. He didn't quite understand what Starke meant. He was too full of the realization that he had just learned what he was for.

Starke had run across carefully rehearsed speeches before. He got at least one a year from some bright boy who'd seen a movie about Young Tom Edison. He knew Martino wasn't likely to be giving him that, but he'd been fooled before. So he took his long look at the boy before he said anything.

He saw Lucas Martino looking back at him as though sixteen-year-old boys took their irrevocable vows every day.

It upset Starke. It made him uncomfortable, and it made him draw back for the first time in his life.

'Well. So that's your idea of physics. Planning to go on to Massachusetts Tech, are you?'

'If I can get the money together. And my grades aren't too high, are they?'

'The grades can be taken care of, if you'll work at it. The semester's not that far gone. And money's no problem. There're all kinds of science scholarships. If you miss on that, you can probably get one of the big outfits like G.E. to underwrite you.'

Martino shook his head. 'It's a three-factor problem. My graduating average won't be that high, no matter what I do the next two years here. And I don't want to be tied to anybody's company, and third, scholarships don't cover everything. You've got to have decent clothes at college, and you've got to have some money in your pocket to relax on once in a while. I've heard about M.I.T. Nobody human can take their curriculum and earn money part-time. If you're there, you're there for twenty-four hours a day. And I'm going for my doctorate. That's seven years, minimum. No, I'm going to New York after I graduate here and work in my Uncle Luke's place until I get some money put away. I'll be a New York resident and put in a cheap year at C.C.N.Y. I'll pile up an average there, and get my tuition scholarship at Massachusetts that way.'

The plan unfolded easily and spontaneously. Starke couldn't have guessed it was being created on the spot. Martino had put all the facts together, seen how they fitted, and what action they indicated. It was as easy as that.

'Talked it over with your parents, have you?'

'Not yet.' For the first time, he showed hesitation. 'It'll be rough on them. It'll be a long time before I can send them any money.' Also, but never to be put in words for a stranger, the life of the family would be changed for ever, never to be put back in the same way again.

2

'I don't understand,' his mother said. 'Why should you suddenly want to go to this school in Boston? Boston is far away from here. Farther than New York.'

He had no easy answer. He sat awkwardly at the dinner table, looking down at his plate.

'I don't understand it either,' his father said to his mother. 'But if he wants to go, that's his choice. He's not leaving right away, in any case. By the time he goes, he'll be a man. A man has a right to decide these things.'

He looked from his mother to his father, and he could see it wasn't something he could explain. For a moment, he almost said he'd changed his mind.

Instead he said, 'Thank you for your permission.' Move one piece of the universe, and all the others are affected. Add something to one piece, and another must lose. What real choice did he have, when everything meshed together, one block of fact against another, and there was only one best way to act?

Chapter 5

On the eighth day after the man had come over the line, the annunciator buzzed on Rogers' desk.

'Yes?'

'Mr Deptford is here to see you, sir.'

Rogers grunted. He said, 'Send him in, please,' and sat waiting.

Deptford came into the office. He was a thin, grey-faced man in a dark suit, and he was carrying a briefcase. 'How are you, Shawn?' he said quietly.

Rogers stood up. 'Fine, thanks,' he answered slowly. 'How are you?'

Deptford shrugged. He sat down in the chair beside the end of Rogers' desk and laid the briefcase in his lap. 'I thought I'd bring the decision on the Martino matter down with me.' He opened the briefcase and handed Rogers a manila envelope. 'In there's the usual file copy of the official policy directive, and a letter to you from Karl Schwenn's office.'

Rogers picked up the envelope. 'Did Schwenn give you a very bad time, sir?'

Deptford smiled thinly. 'They didn't quite know what to do. It didn't seem to be anybody's fault. But they'd needed an answer very badly. Now, at the sacrifice of the K-Eighty-eight programme, they don't need it so badly any more. But they still need it, of course.'

Rogers nodded slowly.

'I'm replacing you here as sector chief. They've put a new man in my old job. And the letter from Schwenn reassigns you to follow up on Martino. Actually, I think Schwenn arrived at the best answer to a complicated situation.'

Rogers felt his lips stretch in an uncomfortable grimace of

surprise and embarrassment. 'Well.' There was nothing else to say.

2

'Direct investigation won't do it,' Rogers said to the man. 'We tried, but it can't be done. We can't prove who you are.'

The glinting eyes looked at him impassively. There was no telling what the man might be thinking. They were alone in the small room, and Rogers suddenly understood that this had turned into a personal thing between them. It had happened gradually, he could see now, built up in small increments over the past days, but this was the first time it had struck him, and so it had also happened suddenly. Rogers found himself feeling personally responsible for the man's being here, and for everything that had happened to him. It was an unprofessional way to feel, but the fact was that he and this man were here face to face, alone, and when it came down to the actual turn of the screw it was Rogers whose hand was on the wrench.

'I see what you mean,' the man said. 'I've been doing a lot of thinking about it.' He was sitting stiffly in his chair, his metal hand across his lap, and there was no telling whether he had been thinking of it coldly and dispassionately, or whether hopes and desperate ideas had gone echoing through his brain like men in prison hammering on the bars. 'I thought I might be able to come up with something. What about skin pore patterns? Those couldn't have been changed.'

Rogers shook his head. 'I'm sorry, Mr Martino. Believe me, we had experts in physical identification thrashing this thing back and forth for days. Pore patterns were mentioned, as a matter of fact. But unfortunately, that won't do us any good. We don't have verified records from before the explosion. Nobody ever thought we'd have to go into details as minute as that.' He raised his hand, rubbed it wearily across the side of his head, and dropped it in resignation. 'That's true of everything in that line, I'm afraid. We have your fingerprints and retinal photographs on file. Both are useless now.'

And here we are, he thought, fencing around the entire question of whether you're really Martino but went over to them. There're limits to what civilized people can bring out into the open, no matter how savagely they can speculate. So it doesn't matter. There's no easy escape for either of us, no matter what we say or do now. We've had our try at the easy answers, and there aren't any. It's the long haul for both of us now.'

'Isn't there anything to work on at all?'

'I'm afraid not. No distinguishing marks or scars that couldn't be faked, no tattoos, no anything. We've tried, Mr Martino. We've thought of every possibility. We accumulated quite a team of specialists. The consensus is there's no fast answer.'

'That's hard to believe,' the man said.

'Mr Martino, you're more deeply involved in the problem than any of us. You've been unable to offer anything useful. And you're a pretty smart man.'

'If I'm Lucas Martino,' the man said dryly.

'Even if you're not.' Rogers brought his palms down on his knees. 'Let's look at it logically. Anything we can think of, they could have thought of first. In trying to establish anything about you, normal approaches are useless. We're the specialists in charge of taking you apart, and a great many of us have been in this kind of work a long time. I was head of A.N.G. Security in this sector for seven years. I'm the fellow responsible for the agents we drop into their organizations. But when I try to crack you, I've got to face the possibility that just as many experts on the other side worked at putting you together – and you yourself can most likely match my own experience in spades. What's opposed here are the total efforts of two efficient organizations, each with the resources of half the world. That's the situation, and we're all stuck with it.'

'What're you going to do?'

'That's what I'm here to tell you. We couldn't keep you here indefinitely. We don't do things that way. So you're free to go.'

The man raised his head sharply. 'There's a catch to it.'

Rogers nodded. 'Yes, there is. We can't let you go back to sensitive work. That's the catch, and you already knew it. Now it's official. You're free to go and do anything you like, as long as it isn't physics.'

'Yes.' The man's voice was quiet. 'You want to see me run.

How long does that injunction apply? How long're you going to keep watching me?'

'Until we find out who you are.'

The man began to laugh, quietly and bitterly.

3

'So he's leaving today?' Finchley asked.

'Tomorrow morning. He wants to go to New York. We're paying his flight transportation, we've assigned him a one hundred per cent disability pension, and given him four months' back pay at Martino's scale.'

'Are you going to put a surveillance team on him in New York?'

'Yes. And I'll be on the plane with him.'

'*You* will? You're dropping your job here?'

'Yes. Orders. He's my personal baby. I'll head up the New York A.N.G. surveillance unit.'

Finchley looked at him curiously. Rogers kept his eyes level. After a moment, the F.B.I. man made an odd sucking noise between his two upper front teeth and let it go at that. But Rogers saw his mouth stretch into the peculiar grimace a man shows when a fellow professional falls from grace.

'What's your procedure going to be?' Finchley asked carefully. 'Just keep him under constant watch until he makes a wrong move?'

Rogers shook his head. 'No. We've got to screw it down tighter than that. There's only one possible means of identification left. We've got to build up a psychological profile on Lucas Martino. Then we'll match it against this fellow's pattern of actions and responses, in situations where we'd be able to tell exactly how the real Martino'd react. We're going to dig – deeper than any security clearance, deeper than the Recording Angel, if we have to. We're going to reduce Lucas Martino to so many points on a graph, and then we're going to chart this fellow against him. Once he does something Lucas Martino would never have done, we'll know. Once he expresses an attitude the old, loyal Lucas Martino didn't have, we'll come down on him like a ton of bricks.'

'Yes – but . . .' Finchley looked uncomfortable. His specific assignment to Rogers' team was over. From now on he'd be only a liaison man between Rogers' A.N.G. surveillance unit and the F.B.I. As a member of a different organization, he'd be expected to give help when needed, but no unasked-for suggestions. And particularly now, with Rogers bound to be sensitive about rank, he was wary of overstepping.

'Well?' Rogers asked.

'Well, what you're going to do is wait for this man to make his mistake. He's a clever man, so he won't make it soon, and it won't be a big one. It'll be some little thing, and it may be years before he makes it. It may be fifteen years. He may die without making it. And all that time he'll be on the spot. All that time he may be Lucas Martino – and if he is, this system's never going to prove it.'

Rogers' voice was soft. 'Can you think of anything better? Anything at all?' It wasn't Finchley's fault they were in this mess. It wasn't the A.N.G.'s fault he'd had to be demoted. It wasn't Martino's fault this whole thing had started. It wasn't Rogers' fault – still, wasn't it? he thought – that Mr Deptford had been demoted. They were caught up in a structure of circumstances that were each fitted to one another in an inevitable pattern, each so shaped and so placed that they fell naturally into a trackless maze, and there was nothing for anyone to do but follow along.

'No,' Finchley admitted, 'I can't see any way out of it.'

4

There was a ground fog at the airfield and Rogers stood outside alone, waiting for it to lift. He kept his back turned to the car parked ten feet away, beside the administration building, where the other man was sitting with Finchley. Rogers' top coat collar was turned up, and his hands were in his pockets. He was staring out at the dirty metal skin of the aeroplane waiting on the apron. He was thinking of how aircraft in flight flashed molten in the sky, dazzling as angels, and how on the ground their purity was marred by countless grease-rimmed rivet heads, by oil stains, by scuff marks where mechanics' feet had slipped, and by droplets of water that dried away each to leave a speck of dirt behind.

He slipped two fingers inside his shirt, like a pick-pocket, and pulled out a cigarette. Closing his thin lips around it, he stood bareheaded in the fog, his hair a corona of beaded moisture, and listened to the public address system announce that the fog was dissipating and passengers were requested to board their planes. He looked through the glass wall of the administration building into the passenger lounge and saw the people there getting to their feet, closing their coats, getting their tickets ready.

The man had to go out into the world sometime. This was an ordinary commercial civilian flight, and sixty-five people, not counting Rogers and Finchley, would be exposed to him at one blow.

Rogers hunched his shoulders, lit his cigarette, and wondered what would happen. The fog seemed to have worked its way into his nasal passages and settled at the back of his throat. He felt cold and depressed. The gate checker came out and took up his position, and people began filing out of the passenger lounge.

Rogers listened for the sound of the car door. When it didn't come at once, he wondered if the man was going to wait until everyone was aboard, in hopes of being able to take the last seat and so, for a little time, avoid being noticed.

The man waited until the passengers were collected in the inevitable knot around the ticket checker. Then he got out of the car, waited for Finchley to slide out, and slammed the door like a gunshot.

Rogers jerked his head in that direction, realizing everyone else was, too.

For a moment, the man stood there holding his overnight bag in one gloved hand, his hat pulled down low over his obscene skull, his top coat buttoned to the neck, his collar up. Then he set the bag down and pulled off his gloves, raising his face to look directly at the other passengers. Then he lifted his metal hand and yanked his hat off.

In the silence he walked forward quickly, hat and bag in his good hand, taking his ticket out of his breast pocket with the other. He stooped, bent, and picked up a woman's handbag.

'I believe you dropped this?' he murmured.

The woman took her purse numbly. The man turned to Rogers and, in a deliberately cheerful voice, said, 'Well, time to be getting aboard, isn't it?'

Chapter 6

Young Lucas came to the city at a peculiar time.

The summer of 1966 was uncomfortable for New York. It was usually cooler than expected, and it often rained. The people who ordinarily spent their summer evenings in the parks, walking back and forth and then sitting down to watch other people walk past, felt disappointed in the year. The grumbling old men who sold ice-cream sticks from three-wheeled carts rang their bells more vigorously than they would have liked. Fewer people came to the band concerts on the Mall in Central Park, and the music, instead of diffusing gently through heat-softened air, had a tinny ring to the practised ear.

There were hot days here and there. There were weeks at a time when it seemed that the weather had settled down at last, and the city, like a machine late in shifting gears but shifting at last, would try to fall into its true summer rhythm. But then it would rain again. The rain glazed the sidewalks instead of soaking into them, and the leaves on the trees curled rather than opened. It would have been a perfectly good enough summer for Boston, but New York had to force itself a little. Everyone was just a fraction on edge, knowing how New York summers ought to be, knowing how you ought to feel in the summer, and knowing that this year just wasn't making it.

Young Lucas Martino knew only that the city seemed to be a nervous, discontented place. His uncle, Lucas Maggiore, who was his mother's older brother and who had been in the States since 1936, was glad enough to see and hire him, but he was growing old and he was moody. *Espresso Maggiore*, where young Lucas was to work from noon to three a.m. each day but Monday, grinding coffee, charging the noisy espresso machine, carrying armfuls of cups to the tables, had until recently been a simple neighbourhood trattoria for the neighbourhood Italians who didn't care to patronize the rival Greek kaffeneikons.

But the tourist area of Greenwich Village had spread down to include the block where Lucas Maggiore had started his coffee house when he stopped wrestling sacks of roasted beans in a restaurant supply warehouse. So now there were murals on the walls, antique tables, music by Muzak, and a new I.B.M. electric cash register. Lucas Maggiore, a big, heavy, indrawn bachelor who had always managed to have enough money, now had more. He was able to pay his only nephew more than he deserved, and still had enough left to make him wonder if perhaps he shouldn't live more freely than he had in the past. But he had an ingrained caution against flying too far in the face of temptation, and so he was moody. He felt a vague resentment against the coffee house, hired a manager, and stayed away most of the time. He began stopping more and more often by the Park Department tables in Washington Square, where old men in black overcoats sat and played checkers with the concentration of chessmasters, and sometimes he was on the verge of asking to play.

When young Lucas came to New York, his uncle had embraced him at Pennsylvania Station, patted him between the shoulder blades, and held him off by both arms to look at him:

'Ah! Lucas! *Bello nipotino! E la Mama, il Papa – come lei portano?*'

'They're fine, Uncle Lucas. They send their love. I'm glad to see you.'

'So. All right – I like you, you like me – we'll get along. Let's go.' He took Lucas' suitcase in one big hand and led the way to the subway station. 'Mrs Dormiglione – my landlady – she has a room for you. Cheap. It's a good room. Nice place. Old lady Dormiglione, she's not much for cleaning up. You'll have to do that yourself. But that way, she won't bother you much. You're young, Lucas – you don't want old people bothering you all the time. You want to be with young people. You're eighteen – you want a little life.' Lucas Maggiore inclined his head in the direction of a passing girl.

Young Lucas didn't quite know what to say. He followed his uncle into a downtown express car and stood holding on to the overhead bar as the train jerked to a start. Finally, having nothing conclusive to say, he said nothing. When the train reached Fourth Street, he and his uncle got off, and went to the furnished rooming house just off West Broadway where Lucas Maggiore lived on the top floor and Lucas Martino was to live in the basement – with an entrance separate from the main front door. After young Lucas had been introduced to Mrs Dormiglione, shown his room, and given a few minutes to put his suitcase away and wash his face, his uncle took him to the coffee house.

On the way there, Lucas Maggiore turned to young Lucas.

'Lucas and Lucas – that's too many Lucases in one store. Does Matteo have another name for you?'

Lucas thought back. 'Well, sometimes Papa calls me Tedeschino.'

'Good! In the store, that's your name. All right?'

'Fine.'

So that was the name by which Lucas was introduced to the employees of *Espresso Maggiore*. His uncle told him to be at work at noon the next day, advanced him a week's pay, and left him. They saw each other occasionally after that, and sometimes when his uncle wanted company, he asked young Lucas whether he would like to eat with him, or listen to music on the phonograph in Mrs Dormiglione's parlour. But Lucas Maggiore had so arranged things that young Lucas had a life of his own, freedom to live it, and was still close enough so that the boy couldn't get into serious trouble. He felt that he'd done his best for the youngster, and he was right.

So Lucas spent his first day in New York with a firm base under his feet, but on his own. He thought that the city could have been pleasanter, but that he was being given a fair chance. He felt a little isolated, but that was something he felt was up to him to handle.

In another year, with a soft summer, he might have found

it easier to slip quickly into the pattern of the city's life. But this year most people had not been lulled into relaxation – this year they took no vacations from the closed-up, preoccupied attitudes of winter, and so Lucas discovered that New Yorkers putting a meal in front of you in a diner, selling you a movie ticket, or rubbing against you on a crowded bus, could each of them be behind an impenetrable wall.

With another uncle, he might have been taken up into a family much like the one he had left behind. In another house, he might have had a room somewhere where people next door soon struck up an acquaintance. But, as everything was, things so combined that what kind of life he lived for the next year and a half was entirely up to him. He recognized the situation, and in his methodical, logical way, began to consider what kind of life he needed.

2

Espresso Maggiore was essentially one large room, with a counter at one end where the espresso machine was and where the clean cups were kept. There were heavy, elaborately carved tables from Venice and Florence, some with marble tops and some not, and besides the murals executed in an Italianate modern style by one of the neighbourhood artists, there were thickly varnished old oil paintings in flaking gilt frames on the walls. There was a sugar bowl on each table, with a small menu card listing the various kinds of coffee served and the small selection of ices and other sweets available. The walls were painted a warm cream-yellow, and the lights were dim. The music played in the background, from speakers concealed in two genuine Cinquecento cupboards, and from time to time one of the steady patrons would find a vaguely Roman bust or statuette – French neoclassic was close enough – which he would donate to the management for the satisfaction of seeing it displayed on a wooden pedestal somewhere in a corner.

The espresso machine dominated the room. When Lucas Maggiore first opened his trattoria, he had bought a second-hand but nearly new modern electric machine, shining in chrome, looking a good deal like the manifold of a liquid-cooled aircraft engine, with *ATALANTO* proclaiming the maker's name in raised block letters across the topmost tube. When the store was redecorated, the new machine was sold to a kaffeneikon and another machine – one of the old gas-fired models – was put up in its place. This was a great vertical cylinder with a bell top, nickel-plated, with the heads of cherubim bolted to its sides and an eagle rampant atop its bell. Rich with its ornamentation, its sides covered by engraved scrollwork, with spigots protruding from its base, the machine sat on the counter and screamed hisses as it forced steam through the charges of coffee. From noon to three a.m. each day except Monday, gathering thickest around midnight, Villagers and tourists crowded *Espresso Maggiore*, sitting in the wire-back chairs, most of them drinking capuccino in preference to true espresso, which is bitter, and interrupting their conversations whenever the machine hissed.

Besides Lucas, there were four other employees of *Espresso Maggiore*.

Carlo, the manager, was a heavy-set, almost unspeaking man of about thirty-five, cut from the same cloth as Lucas Maggiore and hired for that reason. He handled the machine, usually took cash, and supervised the work and cleaning up. He showed Lucas how to grind the coffee, told him to keep the tables wiped and the sugarbowls full, taught him how to wash cups and saucers with the greatest efficiency, and left him alone after that, since the youngster did his work well.

There were three waitresses. Two of them were more or less typical Village girls, one from the Midwest and the other from Schenectady, who were studying drama and came in to work from eight to one. The third waitress was a neighbourhood girl, Barbara Costa, who was about seventeen or eighteen and worked the full shift every day. She was a pretty, thinnish girl who did her work expertly and wasted no time talking to the Village young men, who came in during the afternoons and sat for hours over their one cup of coffee because nobody minded as long as the store wasn't crowded. Because she was there all day, Lucas got to know her better than the other two girls. They got along well, and during the first few days she took the trouble to teach him the tricks of balancing four or five cups at a time, remembering complicated orders, and keeping a running tab in his head. Lucas liked her for her friendliness, respected her skill because it was organized in a way he understood, and was grateful for having one person he could talk to in the rare moments when he felt a desire to do so.

In a month, Lucas had acclimatized himself to the city. He memorized the complicated network of straggling, unnumbered streets below Washington Square, knew the principal subway routes, found a good inexpensive laundry and a delicatessen where he bought what few groceries he felt he needed. He had investigated the registration system and entrance requirements at City College, sent a letter of inquiry to Massachusetts, and registered with the local Selective Service Board, where his grade in the Technical Aptitude Examination gave him his conditional deferment. He'd have to be a registered physical sciences student within a year, but that was what he was in New York for. So, by and large, he had succeeded in arranging his circumstances to fit his needs.

But what his uncle had hinted at on his first day in the city was beginning to turn itself over in Lucas' mind. He sat down and thought it out systematically.

He was eighteen, and at or near his physical peak. His body was an excellently designed mechanism, with definite needs and functions. This particular year was the last even partly free time he could expect for the next eight years.

Yes, he decided, if he was ever going to get himself a girl, there was no better time for it than now. He had the time, the means, and even the desire. Logic pointed the way, and so he began to look around.

Chapter 7

The plane went into its final downward glide over Long Island, slipping into the New York International landing pattern, and the lounge hostess asked Rogers and the man to take their seats.

The man lifted his highball gracefully, set the edge against the lip of his mouth, and finished his drink. He put the glass down, and the grille moved back into place. He dabbed at his chin with a paper cocktail napkin. 'Alcohol is very bad for high-carbon steel, you know,' he remarked to the hostess.

He had spent most of the trip in the lounge, occasionally ordering a drink, smoking at intervals, holding glass or cigarette in his metal hand. The passengers and crew had been forced to grow accustomed to him.

'Yes, sir,' the hostess said politely.

Rogers shook his head to himself. As he followed the man down the aisle to their seats, he said, 'Not if it's stainless steel Mr Martino. I've seen the metallurgical analyses on you.'

'Yes,' the man said, buckling his seatbelt and resting his hands lightly on his kneecaps. 'You have. But that hostess hasn't.' He put a cigarette in his mouth and let it dangle there, unlit, while the plane banked and steadied on its new heading. He looked out of the window beside him. 'Odd,' he said. 'You wouldn't expect it to still be too early for daylight.'

The moment the plane touched the runway, slowed, and began to taxi towards the offloading ramp, the man unfastened his seatbelt and lit his cigarette. 'We seem to be here,' he said conversationally, and stood up. 'It's been a pleasant trip.'

'Pretty good,' Rogers said, unfastening his own belt. He looked towards Finchley across the aisle, and shook his head helplessly as the F.B.I. man raised his eyebrows. There was no doubt about it – whoever this man was, Martino or not, they were going to have a bad time with him.

'Well,' the man said, 'I don't suppose we'll be meeting socially again, Mr Rogers. I hardly know whether it's proper to say good-bye or not.'

Rogers held out his hand wordlessly.

The man's right hand was warm and firm. 'It'll be good to see New York again. I haven't been here in nearly twenty years. And you, Mr Rogers?'

'Twelve, about. I was born here.'

'Oh, were you?' They moved slowly along the aisle towards the rear door, with the man walking ahead of Rogers. 'Then you'll be glad to get back.'

Rogers shrugged uncomfortably.

The man's chuckle was rueful. 'Pardon me – do you know, for a moment I actually forgot this was hardly a pleasure trip for either of us.'

Rogers had no answer. He followed the man down the aisle to where the stewardesses gave them their coats. They stepped out on the escalator, with Rogers' eyes on a level with the top of the man's bare head.

The man half-turned, as though for another casual remark.

The first flashbulb exploded down at the foot of the escalator, and the man recoiled. He stumbled back against Rogers, and for a moment he was pressed against him. Rogers suddenly caught the stale, acrid smell of the perspiration that had been soaking the man's shirt for hours.

There was a cluster of photographers down on the apron, pointing their cameras at the man and firing their flash-guns in a ripple of sharp light.

The man tried to turn on the escalator. His hard hand closed on Rogers' shoulders as he tried to get him out of the way. The gaskets behind his mouth grille were up out of sight. Rogers heard his two food-grinding blades clash together.

Then Finchley somehow got past both of them, clattering down the escalator. He was reaching for his wallet as he went, and then the F.B.I. shield glittered briefly in the puffballs of light. The photographers stopped.

Rogers took a deep breath and pried the man's hand off his

shoulder. 'All right,' he said gently, lowering the hand carefully as though it were no longer attached to anything. 'It's all right, man, it's under control. The damned pilot must have radioed ahead or something. Finchley'll have a talk with the newspaper editors and the wire service chiefs. You won't get spread all over the world.'

The man got his footing back, and stepped unsteadily off the escalator as they reached the ground. He mumbled something that had to be either thanks or a stumbling apology. Rogers was just as glad not to have heard it.

'We'll take care of the news media. The only thing you'll have left to worry about is the people you meet, but from what I've seen you can do a damn fine job of handling those.'

The man's glittering eyes swung on Rogers savagely. 'Just don't watch me too closely,' he growled.

2

Rogers stood in the local A.N.G. Security office that afternoon, massaging his shoulder from time to time while he talked. Twenty-two men sat in orderly rows of class-room chairs facing him, taking notes on standard pads rested on the broad right arms of the chairs.

'All right,' Rogers said in a tired voice. 'You've all got offset copies of the dossier on Martino. It's pretty complete, but that's only where we start. You'll get your individual assignments as you file out, but I want you all to know what the team's supposed to be doing as a whole. Any one of you may come up with something that'll seem unimportant unless we have the whole picture.

'Now – what we want is a diagram of a man, down to the last capillary and – ' his lips twitched – 'rivet. Out of your individual reports, we're going to put together a master description of him that'll tell us everything from the day he was born to the day the lab went up. We want to know what foods he liked, what cigarettes he smoked, what vices he had, what kind of women he favoured – and why. We want a list of the books he's read – and what he agreed with in them. Almost all of you are going to do nothing but intensive research on him. When we're through, we want to have read a man's mind.' Rogers let his hand fall to his side. 'Because his mind is all we have left to recognize him by.

'Some of you are going to be assigned to direct surveillance. It'll be your reports we'll check against the research. They'll have to be just as detailed, just as precise. Remember that he knows you're watching. That means his gross actions may very well be intended to mislead you. It'll be the small things that might trip him up. Watch who he talks to – but pay just as much attention to the way he lights his cigarettes.

'But remember you're dealing with a genius. He's either Lucas Martino or a Soviet ringer, but, whichever it is, he's sharper than any one of us. You'll have to face that, keep it in mind, and just remember there're more of us and we've got the system. Of course' – Rogers heard the frustrated undertone in his voice – 'he may be part of a system, too. But it'd be much smarter of them to let him go it alone.

'As to what he's here for if he is a ringer: it might be anything. They might seriously have expected him to get back into the technological development programme. If so, he's in a hole right now, with no place to go. He may make a break to get out of the Allied Sphere. Watch out for that. Again, he may be here for something else, figuring the Soviets expected us to handle him just the way we have. If so, there're all kinds of rabbits he could start pulling out of his hat. We're positive he isn't a human bomb or a walking arsenal full of hidden death-rays and other stuff out of the funnies. We're positive, but, Lord knows, we could be wrong. Watch out for him if he starts trying to buy electronic parts, or *anything* he could build something out of.

'Those of you who're going to dig into his history – if he ever fiddled with things in his cellar, or tossed an idea for some kind of nasty gimmick into a discussion, I want to hear about it quick. I don't know what this K-Eighty-eight thing he worked up was – I do know it must have had an awful punch. I think we'd all appreciate it if he didn't put one together in a back room somewhere.'

Rogers sighed. 'All right. Questions?'

A man raised his hand. 'Mr Rogers?'

'Yes.'

56

'How about the other end of this problem? I presume there're teams in Europe trying to penetrate the Soviet organization that worked on him?'

'There are. But they're only doing it because we're supposed to cover all loose ends for the record. They're not getting anywhere. The Soviets have a fellow named Azarin who's their equivalent to a sector security chief. He's good at his work. He's a stone wall. If we get anything out past him, it'll be pure luck. If I know him, everybody connected in any way with whatever happened is in Uzbekistan by now, and the records have been destroyed – if they were ever kept. I know one thing – we had some people I thought I'd planted over there. They're gone. Other questions?'

'Yes, sir. How long do you think it'll be before we can say for sure about this fellow?'

Rogers simply looked at the man.

3

Rogers was sitting alone in his office when Finchley came in. It was growing dark again outside, and the room was gloomy in spite of the lamp on Rogers' desk. Finchley took a chair and waited while Rogers folded his reading glasses and put them back in his breast pocket.

'How'd you make out?' Rogers asked.

'I covered them all. Press, newsreel, and T.V. He's not going to get publicity.'

Rogers nodded. 'Good. If we'd let him become a seven days' wonder, we'd have lost our last chance. It'll be tough enough as it is. Thanks for doing all the work, Finchley. We'd never have got any accurate observations on him.'

'I don't think he'd have enjoyed it, either,' Finchley said.

Rogers looked at him for a moment, and then let it pass. 'So as far as anyone connected with the news media is concerned, this isn't any higher up than F.B.I. level?'

'That's right. I kept the A.N.G. out of it.'

'Fine. Thanks.'

'That's one of the things I'm here for. What did Martino do after what happened at the airport?'

'He took a cab downtown and got off at the corner of Twelfth Street and Seventh Avenue. There's a luncheonette there. He had a hamburger and a glass of milk. Then he walked down to Greenwich Avenue, and down Greenwich to Sixth Avenue. He went down Sixth to Fourth Street. As of a few hours ago, he was walking back and forth on those streets down there.'

'He went right out in public again. Just to prove he hadn't lost his nerve.'

'It looks that way. He stirred up a mild fuss – people turning around to look at him, and a few people pointing. That was all there was to that. It wasn't anything he couldn't ignore. Of course, he hasn't looked for a place to stay yet, either. I'd say he was feeling a little lost right now. The next report's due within the next half hour – sooner if something drastic happens. We'll see. We're checking out the luncheonette.'

Finchley looked up from his chair. 'You know this whole business stinks, don't you?'

'Yes.' Rogers frowned. 'What's that got to do with it?'

'You saw him on the plane. He was dying by inches, and it never showed. He put himself up in front of sixty-odd people and rubbed their faces in what he was, just to prove to himself and to us, and to them, too, that he wasn't going to crawl into a hole. He fooled them, and he fooled us. He looks like nothing that ever walked this earth, and he proved he was as good a man as any of us.'

'We knew that all along.'

'And then, just when he'd done it, the world came up and hit him too hard. He saw himself being spread all over the whole Allied world in full-page colour, and he saw himself being branded a freak for good and all. Well, who hasn't been hit too hard to stand? It's happened to me in my life, and I guess it's happened to you.'

'I imagine it has.'

'But he got up from it. He put himself on the sidewalk for everybody in New York to look at, and he got away with it. He knew what being hit felt like, and he went back for more. That's a man, Rogers – God damn it, that's a man!'

'What man?'

58

'Damn it, Rogers, give them a little time and the right chance, and there isn't an ID the Soviets couldn't fake! We don't have a man they couldn't replace with a ringer if they really wanted to. Nobody – nobody in this whole world – can prove who he is, but we're expecting this one man to do it.'

'We have to. You can't do anything about it. This one man has to prove who he is.'

'He could have just been put somewhere where he'd be harmless.'

Rogers stood up and walked over to the window. His fingers played with the blind cord. 'No man is harmless anywhere in this world. He may sit and do nothing, but he's there, and every other man has to solve the problem of who he is and what he's thinking, because until that problem's solved, that man is dangerous.

'The A.N.G. could have decided to put this man on a desert island, yes. And he might never have done anything. But the Soviets may have the K-Eighty-eight. And the real Martino might still be on their side of the line. By that much, this man on his desert island might be the most dangerous man in the world. And until we get evidence, that's exactly what he is, and equally so no matter where he is. If we're ever going to get evidence, it's going to be here. If we don't get it, then we'll stay close enough to stop him if he turns out not to be our Martino. That's the job, Finchley, and neither you nor I can get out of it. Neither of us'll be old enough for retirement before he dies.'

'Look, damn it, Rogers, I know all that! I'm not trying to crawl out of the job. But we've been watching this man ever since he came back over the line. We've watched him, we've seen what he's going through – damn it, it's not going to make any difference in my work, but as far as I'm concerned – '

'You think he's Martino?'

Finchley stopped. 'I don't have any evidence for it.'

'But you can't help thinking he's Martino. Because he bleeds? Because he'd cry if he had tears. Because he's afraid, and desperate, and knows he has no place to go?' Rogers' hands jerked at the blind cord. 'Don't we all? Aren't we all human beings?'

Chapter 8

Young Lucas Martino turned away from the freshly cleaned table, holding four dirty cups and saucers in his left hand, each cup in its saucer the way Barbara had taught him, with two saucers held overlapping between his fingers and the other two sets stacked on top. He carried his wiping sponge in his right hand, ready to clean up any dirty spots on tables he passed on the way back to the counter. He liked working this way – it was efficient, it wasted no time, and it made no real difference that there was plenty of time, now that the late afternoon rush was over.

He wondered what created these freak rushes, as he set the cups and saucers down in the basket under the counter, first flipping the spoons into a smaller tray. There was no overt reason why, on indeterminate days, *Espresso Maggiore* should suddenly become crowded at four o'clock. Logically, people ought to have been working, or looking forward to supper, or walking in the park on a beautiful day like this. But, instead, they came here – all of them at almost the same time – and for half an hour, the store was crowded. Now, at a quarter of five, it was empty again, and the chairs were once more set in order against the clean tables. But it had been a busy time – so busy, with only Barbara and himself on shift, that Carlo had waited on some tables himself.

He looked at the stacks of dirty cups in the basket. There was a strong possibility, it seemed to him, that most of the customers had ordered the same thing, as well. Not capuccino, for a change, but plain espresso, and that was curious, too, as though a majority of people in the neighbourhood had felt a need for a stimulant, rather than something sweet to drink.

But they all did different things – some were tavern-keepers, some were their employees, some were artists, some were idlers, some were tourists. Were there days when everyone simply grew tired, no matter what they did? Lucas frowned to himself. He tried to recall if he'd ever felt anything of the sort in himself. But one case provided no conclusive evidence. He'd have to file it away and think about it – check back when it happened again.

He let the thought drift to the back of his mind as Barbara cleaned up the last of her tables and came to the counter. She smiled ruefully, shook her head, and wiped her forehead with the back of her wrist. 'Whew! Be glad when this day's over, Tedeschino?'

Lucas grinned. 'Wait'll the night rush.' He watched her bend to add her cups to the basket, and he blushed faintly as her uniform skirt tightened over her slight hips. He caught himself, and hastily pulled out the silverware tray to take into the small back room where the sink was.

'Night rush me no night rushes, Ted. Alice and Gloria'll be here – it won't be half as bad.' Barbara winked at him. 'I bet you'll be glad to see that Alice.'

'Alice? Why?' Alice was an intense, sharp-faced girl who barely paid attention to her work and none at all to either the customers or the people she worked with.

Barbara put the tip of her tongue in her cheek and looked down at the floor. 'Oh, I don't know,' she said, pursing her lips. 'But she was telling me just yesterday how much she liked you.'

Lucas frowned over that. 'I didn't know you and Alice talked to each other that much.' It didn't sound like Alice at all. But he'd have to think about it. If it was true, it meant trouble. Getting involved with a girl where you worked never made sense – or so he'd heard, and he could plainly see the logic of it. Besides, he knew exactly what kind of girl he wanted for his present purposes. It couldn't be anybody he'd fall in love with – Alice fitted that part of it well enough – but she also had to be fairly easy, because his time was limited, and she had to live far enough away so he'd never see her during the ordinary course of the day, when he'd be working or studying.

'You don't like Alice, huh?'

'What makes you say that?' He kept his eyes off Barbara's face.

'You got a look. Your eyes looked like you were thinking of something complicated, and your mouth got an expression that showed you didn't like it.'

'You watch me pretty close, don't you?'

'Maybe. All right, if Alice doesn't suit, how about Gloria? Gloria's pretty.'

'And not very bright.' His girl would at least have to be somebody he could talk to sometimes.

'Well. You don't like Alice, you don't like Gloria – who do you like? Got a girl tucked away somewhere? Going to take her out tomorrow? Tomorrow's the big day to howl, you know. Monday.'

Lucas shrugged. He knew. For the past three Mondays, he'd been cruising the city. 'No. I hadn't even thought about the store being closed tomorrow, to tell you the truth.'

'We got paid today, didn't we? Don't think *I* didn't know it. Mmm, boy – big date tomorrow, and everything.'

Lucas felt his mouth twitch. 'Steady boy?'

'Not yet, But he may be – he just may. Tell you what it is – he's the nicest fellow I ever had take me out. Smooth, good dancer, polite, and grown up. A girl doesn't meet very many fellows like that. When one comes along, she kind of gets taken up with him. But you wonder, sometimes, if you waited a little longer, maybe somebody nicer would come along – if you gave him a chance.' She looked squarely at Lucas. 'I guess you can imagine how it is.'

'Yes – well, I guess I can.' He gnawed his upper lip, looking down, and then blurted out, 'I have to wash these now.' He turned, carrying the silverware tray, and walked quickly into the back room. He spilled the silverware into the sink, slammed the hot water handle over, and stood staring down, his hands curled over the edge of the sink. But after a little while he felt better, even though he could not bring himself to ignore the thought of Barbara having a steady.

By all logic, Barbara was the wrong girl.

62

On that particular Monday, the weather held good. The sun shone down just warmly enough to make the streets comfortable, and the narrow Village sidewalks were crowded by the chairs that the old people sat on beside their front stoops, talking to each other and their old friends passing by. The younger men who did not have to go to work leaned against parked cars and sat on their fenders, and the Village girls walked by self-consciously. People brought their dogs out on the grass of Washington Square Park, and on the back streets there was laundry drying on the lines strung between fire escapes. The handball and tennis courts in the Parks Department enclosure were busy.

Lucas Martino came up to the street from his apartment a little past two-thirty, wearing a light shirt and trousers, and stepped into the midst of this life. He walked head down to the subway station, not looking to either side, feeling restless and troubled. He hoped he'd find the right girl today, and at the same time he was nervous about how he'd approach her. He'd observed the manner in which the high school operators had handled the problem, and he was fairly confident of his ability to do as well. Furthermore, he had once or twice taken a girl to the movies, so he was not a complete novice at the particular social code that applied to girls and young men. But it was not a social partner he was looking for.

There was the matter of Barbara, as well, and it seemed that only self-discipline would be of any use there. He could not afford to become involved with any sort of long-term thing. He could not afford to leave a girl waiting while he went through all the years of training that were ahead of him. And after that, with this business in Asia last year, it looked very much as though, more than ever, any physical sciences specialist would go into government work. It meant a long time of living on a project base somewhere, with limited housing facilities and very little time for anything but work. He knew himself – once started working, he would plunge into it to the exclusion of everything else.

No, he thought, remembering his mother's look when he told her he was going to New York. No, a man with people depending on him had no choice, often, but to hurt either them or himself – and many times, both. Barbara couldn't be asked to place herself in a situation like that.

Besides, he reminded himself, that wasn't what he was looking for now. That wasn't what he needed.

He reached the subway station and took an uptown train to Columbus Circle, and not until he reached there did he raise his head and begin looking at girls.

He walked slowly into Central Park, moving in the general direction of Fifth Avenue. He walked a little self-consciously, sure that at least some of the people sitting on the benches must wonder what he was doing.

There were quite a few girls out in the park, mostly in pairs, and they paid him no attention. Most of them were walking towards the roller-skating rink, where he imagined they would have prearranged dates, or else were hoping to meet a pair of young men. He toyed with the notion of going down to the rink himself, but there was something so desperately purposeless in skating around and around in a circle to sticky organ music that he dropped the idea almost immediately. Instead, he cut up another path and skirted the bird sanctuary, without knowing what it was or what the high fence was for. When he suddenly saw a peacock step out into a glade, spreading its plumes like an unfolding dream, he stopped, entranced. He stood motionless for ten minutes before the bird walked away. Then he unlocked his fingers from the steel mesh and resumed his slow walk, still moving east.

The park was full of people in the clear sunshine. Every row of benches he passed was crowded, baby carriages jutting out into the path and small children trotting after the pigeons. Nursemaids sat talking together in white huddles, and old men read newspapers. Old women in black sat with their purses in their laps, looking out across the lake and working their empty fingers as though they were sewing.

There were a few girls out walking alone. He looked at them cautiously, out of the corners of his eyes, but there wasn't one who looked right for him. He always turned his head to the side of the path and walked by them quickly, or else he stopped and looked carefully at his wristwatch while they passed him in the other direction.

He felt that the right kind of girl for him ought to have a look about her – a way of dressing, or walking, or looking around, that would be different from most girls. It seemed logical to him that a girl who would let strange young men speak to her in the park would have a special kind of attitude, a mark of identification that he couldn't describe but would certainly recognize. And, once or twice in his wanderings around the city, he had thought he'd found a girl like that. But when he walked closer to one of these girls, she was always chewing gum, or had thick orange lipstick, or in some other way gave him a peculiar feeling in the pit of his stomach that made him walk by her as quickly as he could without attracting attention.

Finally, he reached the zoo. He walked back and forth in front of the lion cages for a time. Then he went into the cafeteria and had a glass of milk, taking it outside and sitting at one of the tables on the terrace while he looked down at the seals in their pool. He was feeling increasingly awkward, as he usually did on one of these expeditions, and he took a long time over his milk. He looked at his watch again, and this time it was three-thirty. He had to look at his watch twice, because it seemed to him that he'd been in the park much longer than that. He lit a cigarette, smoked it down to the end, and found that this had taken only five minutes.

He stirred restlessly on the metal chair. He ought to get up and start moving around again, but he was haunted by the certainty that if he did that, his feet would carry him right out of the park and back to the downtown subway.

He ran his fingers over his forehead. He was sweating. There was a woman sitting at the next table, drinking iced tea. She was about thirty-five, he would have judged, dressed in expensive-looking clothes. She looked at him peculiarly, and he dropped his glance. He stood up, pushing his chair back with a harsh rattle of its legs on the terrace stones, and walked quickly down into the plaza where the seal tank was.

He watched the seals for a few minutes, his hands closed

over the fence rail. The thought that he was on the verge of giving the whole thing up bothered him tremendously.

He had thought this business out, after all, and come to a logical decision. He had always abided by his decisions before, and they had invariably worked out well.

It was this Barbara business, he decided. There was nothing wrong with being in love with her – there was plenty of room for illogic in his logic – but it was bound to complicate his immediate plan. Yet, it was obvious that there was nothing he could do but to go ahead in spite of it. Barbara, or a girl like Barbara, would come later, when he had settled his life down. That all belonged in a different compartment of his mind, and ought not to be crossing over into this one.

It was the first time in his life that he found himself unable to do what he ought to do, and it bothered him deeply. It made him angry. He turned abruptly away from the seal tank and marched up the steps back towards the exit beyond the lion cages.

While he'd been drinking his milk, a girl had set up a camp stool in front of the cages and was sitting on it, sketching. He noticed her out of the corner of his eye, walked up to her, and without even having bothered to particularly look at her, said challengingly, 'Haven't I seen you some place before?'

3

The girl was about his own age, with very pale blonde hair that was straight, cut close to her skull, and tapered at the back of the neck. She had high cheekbones with hollows under them, a thin nose, and a broad, full mouth which she did not lipstick to the corners. Her eyebrows were very thick and black, painted in with some gummy black cosmetic that looked like stage make-up more than eyebrow pencil. She was wearing flat balletish slippers, a full printed skirt and a peasant blouse. Her eyes were brown and a little startled.

Lucas realized that it was impossible to know what she really looked like, that she was probably quite plain, and, furthermore, that she was far from a girl he could even like. He saw that the sketch she was working on was completely lifeless. It was a fair enough rendering of a lioness, but it felt like a picture of something stuffed and carefully arranged in a window.

He felt angry at her for her looks, for her lack of talent, and for being there. 'No, I suppose not,' he said, and turned to walk away.

'You may have,' the girl said. 'My name's Edith Chester. What's yours?'

He stopped. Her voice was surprisingly gentle, and the very fact that she had reacted in any calm way at all was enough to make him feel like an idiot. 'Luke,' he said, and, for some reason, shrugged.

'Are you at the Art Student's League?' she asked.

He shook his head. 'No. I'm not.' He stopped, and then, just as she was opening her mouth to say something else, he blurted, 'As a matter of fact, I don't know you at all. I was just –' He stopped again, feeling more foolish than ever, and getting angry again.

Surprisingly, now, she had a nervous laugh. 'Well, that's all right, I guess. You're not going to bite my head off, are you?'

The association of ideas was fairly obvious. He looked down at her sketch pad and said, 'That's not much of a lioness.'

She looked at the drawing too, and said, 'Well, no, I suppose it isn't.'

He had wanted to draw a hostile reaction out of her – to start an argument he could walk away on. Now he was in deeper than ever, and he had no idea of what to do. 'Look – I was going to the movies. You want to come along?'

'All right,' she said, and once again he was trapped.

'I was going to see *Queen of Egypt*,' he declared, picking a picture as far as possible from the taste of anyone with pretensions to intelligence.

'I haven't seen that,' she said. 'I wouldn't mind.' She dropped her pencils into her purse, put the sketch pad under her arm, and folded the camp stool. 'We can leave all this stuff at the League,' she said. 'Would you mind carrying the stool for me? It's only a couple of blocks from here.'

He took it without a word, and the two of them walked out of the park together. As they crossed the plaza, going towards the Fifth Avenue exit, he looked over towards the terrace in front of the cafeteria, but the stylishly dressed woman who'd sat at the next table was gone.

He stood in front of the League building, smoking, and waiting for the girl to come out. He didn't know what to do.

The thought of walking around the corner and taking a downtown bus had occurred to him. His hand in his pocket had already found the quarter for the farebox. But it was obvious by now that he'd picked on a girl not very many boys could be interested in, and that if he walked out on her now, he'd be hurting her badly. This whole thing wasn't her fault – he wished it was – and the only thing to do was to go through with it. So he waited for her, flipping the quarter angrily in his pocket, and in due course she came out.

By now he was feeling ashamed of himself. She came out quickly, and when she saw him, she smiled for the first time since he'd met her – a smile that transformed her face for a moment before she remembered not to show relief at his still being there. Then she dropped her eyes in quick decorum. 'I'm ready.'

'All right.' Now he was annoyed again. She was so easy to read that he resented the lack of effort. He wanted someone with depth – someone he could come to know over a long period of time, someone whose total self could be unfolded gradually, would be always interesting and never quite completely explored. Instead, he had Edith Chester.

And yet it wasn't her fault. It was his, and he ought to be shot.

'Look – ' he said, 'you don't want to see that phony Egyptian thing.' He nodded across the street to where one of the expensive, quality movie houses was showing a European picture. 'How about going to see that, instead?'

'If you want to, I'd like that.'

And she was so damned ready to follow his lead! He almost tested her by changing his mind again, but all he did was to say 'Let's go, then,' and start across the street. She followed

68

him immediately, as though she hadn't expected him to wait for her.

She waited at the lobby doors as he bought the tickets, and sat quietly beside him throughout the entire picture. He made no move to hold her hand or put his arm on the back of her seat, and halfway through the picture he suddenly realized that he wouldn't know what to do with her after the picture was over. It would be too early to take her home and thank her for the lovely evening, and yet too late simply to leave her adrift, even if he could think of some graceful way of doing it. He was tempted simply to excuse himself, get up, and walk out of the theatre. Somehow, for all its clumsiness and cruelty, that seemed like the best thing to do. But he held the thought for only a few seconds before he realized he couldn't do it.

Why not? he thought. Am I such a wonderful fellow that it'd blight her life for ever?

But it wasn't that. It wasn't what he was, it was what she was. He could have been the hunchback of Notre Dame and this same situation would still exist. He had put her in it, and it was up to him to see she wasn't hurt as the result of something he'd done.

But what was he going to do with her? He chain-smoked angrily through the rest of the picture, shifting back and forth in his seat.

The picture reached the scene where they'd come in, and she leaned over. 'Do you want to go now?'

Her voice, after ninety minutes of silence, startled him. It was as gentle as it had been when he first spoke to her – before the realization of what was happening had quite come home to her. Now, he supposed, she'd had time to grow calm again.

'All right.' He found himself reluctant to leave. Once out on the street, the awkward, inevitable 'What'll we do now?' would come, and he had no answer. But he stood up and they left the theatre.

Standing under the marquee, she said, 'It was a good picture, wasn't it?'

He pushed the end of a cigarette into his mouth, preoccupied. 'Do you have go to go home now, or anything?' he mumbled around it.

She shook her head. 'No, I live by myself. But you've probably got something to do tonight. I'll just catch a bus here. Thank you for taking me to the movie.'

'No – no, that's all right,' he said quickly. Damn it, she'd been *expecting* him to try and get rid of her. 'Don't do that.' And now he had to propose something for them to do. 'Are you hungry?'

'A little.'

'All right, then, let's go find some place to eat.'

'There's a very good delicatessen just around the corner.'

'All right.' For some reason, he took her hand. It was small, but not fragile. She seemed neither surprised nor shocked. Wondering what the devil had made him do that, he walked with her down to the delicatessen.

The place was still fairly empty, and he led her to a booth in the back. They sat down facing each other, and a waiter came and took their orders. When he left, Lucas realized he should have thought of what would happen when he came in here with her.

They were cut off. The high plywood back behind him separated them from the rest of the room. On one side of them was a wall, and on the other, barely leaving people clearance to slide in and out of the booth's far seat, was an air conditioner. He had let himself and the girl be manoeuvred into a pocket where they had nothing to do but sit and stare at each other while they waited for their food.

What was there to do or say? Looking at that hair-do and the metallic pink polish on her nails, he couldn't imagine what she could possibly talk about, or like, that he could find the faintest interest in.

'Have you been in the city long?' he asked.

She shook her head. 'No, I haven't.'

That seemed to be that.

He'd thrown his cigarette away, somewhere. He knocked a fresh one out of the packet in his shirt pocket and lit it, wishing the waiter would hurry up so they could at least eat. He stole a glance at his watch. It was only six o'clock.

'Could – could I have a cigarette, please?' she asked, her voice and expression uncertain, and he jumped.

'What?' He thrust the packet out clumsily. 'Oh –gee, Edith, I'm sorry! Sure – here. I didn't . . .' Didn't what? Didn't even offer her the courtesy of a cigarette. Didn't stop to wonder whether she smoked or not. Treated her as if she was a pet dog.

He felt peculiarly embarrassed and guilty. Worse, now, than ever before.

She took the cigarette and he lit it for her quickly.

She smiled a little nervously. 'Thank you. I come from Connecticut, originally. Where're you from, Luke?'

She must've known how I felt about her, he was thinking. It must have been sticking out all over me. But she let me go on, because . . . Because why? Because I'm the man of her dreams?

'New Jersey,' he said. 'From a farm.'

'I always wished I could live on a farm. Are you working here?'

Because I'm probably the first guy that's talked to her since she got here, that's why. I may not be much, but I'm all she's got.

'I am for the time being. I work for an espresso house down in the Village.'

He realized he was starting to tell her things he hadn't intended to. But he had to talk, now, and besides, this wasn't what he'd planned – not at all.

'I've only been down there once or twice,' she said. 'It must be a fascinating place.'

'I guess it is, in a way. I'm going to be starting school next year, though, and I won't be seeing much of it.'

'Oh – what're you going to study, Luke?'

So it came out, bit by bit, more and more fluently. They talked while they ate, and words seemed to jump out of him. He told her about the farm, and about high school, and about the espresso house.

They finished eating and went for a walk, up Central Park South and then turning uptown, and he continued to talk. She walked beside him, her feet in their slippers making soft, padding sounds on the asphalt pavement.

After a while, it was time to take her home. She lived on the

West Side, near the gas plant in the Sixties, on the third floor of a tenement. He walked her upstairs, to her door, and suddenly he was out of talk.

He stopped, as abruptly as he'd started, and stood looking down at her, wondering what the devil had got into him. The roots of her hair were very dark, he saw.

'I've been bending your ear,' he said uncomfortably.

She shook her head. 'No. No, you're a very interesting person. I didn't mind at all. It's – ' She looked up at him, and dropped even the minimum of pretence that she had managed to keep throughout the afternoon and evening. 'It's nice to have somebody talk to me.'

He had nothing to say to that. They stood in front of her door, and the silence grew between them.

'I had a very good time,' she said at last.

No, you didn't, he thought. You had a miserable time. The worst thing that ever happened to you was when I spoke to you in front of the lion cages. And now I'm going to walk down those stairs and never call you up or see you again, and that'll be worse, I guess. I've really messed things up. 'Look – have you got a phone?' he found himself saying.

She nodded quickly. 'Yes, I do. Would you like the number?'

'I'll write it down.' He found a peice of paper in his wallet and a pencil in his shirt pocket. He wrote the number down, put his wallet and his pencil back, and once again they simply stood there.

'Monday's my day off,' he said. 'I'll call you.'

'All right, Luke.'

He looked down at her, thinking, No, no, God damn it, I'm not going to try and kiss her goodnight. This isn't like that. This is a crazy thing. She's not like that.

'Goodnight, Edith.'

'Goodnight, Luke.'

He reached out and touched her shoulder, feeling as though he had a stupid expression on his face. She put her hand up and covered his. Then he turned away and went quickly down the stairs, feeling like a fool, and a savage, and an idiot, and like almost anything but an eighteen-year-old boy.

When he went to work the next day, he was all mixed up. No matter how much he thought about it, he couldn't make sense out of what happened to him yesterday. He went about his work in an abstract daze, his mind so knotted that his face was completely blank. He avoided Barbara's eyes, and tried to keep from talking to her.

Finally, in the middle of the afternoon, she trapped him behind the counter. He stood there hopelessly, caught between the espresso machine and the cash register, an emptied cup dangling from his hand.

Barbara smiled at him pleasantly. 'Hey, there, Tedesco, thinking about your money?' There was an anxious tightness in the skin at the corners of her eyes.

'Money?'

'Well – you know. When somebody goes around in a fog, people usually ask him if he's thinking about his money.'

'Oh! No – no, it's not anything like that.'

'What'd you do yesterday? Fall in love?'

His face turned hot. The cup almost dropped out of his hand, as though he were an automatic machine and Barbara had struck a button. And then he was astonished at his reaction to the word. He stood gaping, completely off-stride.

'I'll be damned,' Barbara said. 'I hit it.'

Lucas had no clear idea of what to say. Fall in love? *No!* 'Look – Barbara – it's not ... *that* way ...'

'What way?' Her cheekbones were splotched with red.

'I don't know. I'm just trying to explain ...'

'Look, *I* don't care what way it is. If it's giving you trouble, I hope you get it straightened out. But I've got a fellow who gives *me* trouble, now and then.'

As she thought about it, she realized she was being perfectly honest. She remembered that Tommy was a nice guy, and interesting too. It was a shame about Lucas, because she'd always thought he'd be nice to go out with, but that was the way things worked out: you got a certain fair share of good breaks from life, and you had no right to expect things your way every time.

She was already closing down her mind to any possibility that there might have been more than a few friendly dates between them. She was a girl with a great deal of common sense, and she had learned that there was nothing to be gained in life from idle second thoughts.

'Well, rush hour's coming up,' she said pointedly, got the sugar can out from under the counter, and went to refill the bowls on her tables. Her heels tapped rapidly on the wooden floor.

For a long moment, Lucas was only beginning to get his thoughts in order. The whole business had happened so fast.

He looked towards where Barbara was busy with her tables, and it was obvious to him that as far as she was concerned, the whole episode was over.

Not for him. It was barely beginning. Now it had to be analysed – gone over, dissected, thoroughly examined for every possible reason why things had worked out this way. Only yesterday morning he had been a man with a definite course of action in mind, based on a concrete and obvious situation.

Now everything was changed, in such a short space of time, and it was unthinkable that anyone could simply leave it at that, without asking how, and why.

And yet Barbara was obviously doing just that – accepting a new state of affairs without question or investigation.

Lucas frowned at the problem. It was an interesting thing to think over.

It was even more than that, though he was at best partially aware of it. It was a perfect problem to consider if he didn't want to think about the way he felt towards Edith.

He stood behind the counter, thinking that all the people he had ever known – even people fully as quick-minded as Barbara – consistently took things as they came. And it struck him that if so many people were that way, then there must be value in it. It was actually a far simpler way of living – less wasteful of time, more efficient in its use of emotional energy, more direct.

Then, it followed that there was something inefficient and

basically wrong with his whole approach to living among other people. It was no surprise he'd fallen into this emotional labyrinth with Barbara and Edith.

Now his mind had brought him back to that. How *did* he feel about Edith? He couldn't just forget about it. He'd asked for her phone number. She'd be expecting him to call. He could see her, quite plainly, waiting at night for the phone to ring. He had a responsibility there.

And Barbara. Well – Barbara was tough-fibred. But he must have hurt her at least a little bit.

But how had this whole business come about? In one day, he'd made a mess of everything. It might be easy to simply forget it and start fresh, but could he do that? Could he let something like this stay in the back of his mind forever, unresolved?

I'm all fouled up, he thought.

He had thought he understood himself, and he had shaped himself to live most efficiently in his world. He had made plans on that basis, and seen no flaws in them. But now he had to re-learn almost everything before a new and better Lucas Martino could emerge.

For one more moment before he had to get to work, he tried to decide how he could puzzle it all out and still learn not to waste his time analysing things that couldn't be changed. But rush hour was coming. People were already starting to trickle into the store, and his tables weren't set up yet.

He had to leave it at that, but not permanently. He pushed it to the back of his mind, where he could bring it out and worry at it when he had time – where it could stay for ever, unchanging and waiting to be solved.

6

Circumstances trapped him. Soon he was in school. There he had to learn to give precisely the answers expected of him, and no others. He learned, and there was no difficulty about the scholarship to Massachusetts Tech. But that demanded a great deal of his attention.

He saw Edith fairly often. Whenever he called her, it was

always with the hope that *this* time something would happen – they'd fight, or elope, or do something dramatic enough to solve things at one stroke. Their dates were always nerve-racking for that reason, and they were never casual with each other. He noticed that she gradually let her hair grow out dark brown, and that she stopped living on her parents' cheques. But he had no idea of what that might mean. She found work in a store on Fourteenth Street, and moved into a nearby cold-water flat where they sometimes visited together. But he had manoeuvred himself into a position where every step he made to solve one problem only made the other worse. So he wavered between them. He and Edith rarely even kissed. They never made love.

He stayed on at *Espresso Maggiore* until his studies began taking up too much of his time. He often talked to Barbara through slack times in the day. But they were just two people working in the same place and helping each other fight boredom. The only things they could talk about were the work, his studies, or what would happen to her fiancé now that the Allied Nations Government had been formed and American men might well find themselves as replacements at Australian technical installations. Never, with anyone, could he talk about anything important.

In the fall of 1968 he left New York for Boston. He had not been working since January, and had fallen out of touch with his uncle and Barbara. His relationship with Edith was such that he had nothing to write letters about. They exchanged Christmas cards for a few years.

The work at Tech. was exhausting. Fifty per cent of every freshman class was not expected to graduate, and those who intended to stay found themselves with barely enough time to sleep. Lucas rarely left the campus. He went through three years of undergraduate work, and then continued towards his Master's and his Doctorate. For seven years he lived in exactly the same pocket universe.

Before he ever even got his Master's degree, he saw the beginning of the logic chain that was to end in the K-Eighty-eight. When he received his Doctorate, he was immediately assigned to an American government research project and lived for years on one research reservation after another, none of them substantially different from the academic campus. He was consistently deferred from military service. When he submitted his preliminary paper on the K-Eighty-eight field effect, he was transferred to an identical A.N.G. installation. When his experimental results proved to be worth further work, he was given his own staff and laboratory, and, again, he was not free of schedules, routines, and restricted areas. Though he was free to think, he had only one world to grow in.

While still at M.I.T., he had been sent Edith's wedding announcement. He added the fact to the buried problem, and, with that one change, it lay carefully safeguarded by his perfect memory, waiting, through twenty years, for his first free time to think.

Chapter 9

It was almost eight o'clock at night. Rogers put down his office phone and looked over towards Finchley. 'He stopped for a hamburger and coffee at a Nedick's on the corner of Eighth Street and Sixth Avenue. But he still hasn't talked to anybody, been anywhere in particular, or looked for a place to stay. He's still walking. Still wandering.'

Rogers thought to himself that at least the man had eaten. Rogers and Finchley hadn't. On the other hand, the two of them were sitting down, while, with every step the man took on the concrete sidewalk, two hundred and sixty-eight pounds fell on his already ruined feet. Then, why was he walking? Why didn't he stop? He'd been up since before dawn in Europe, and yet he kept going.

Finchley shook his head. 'I wonder why he's doing that? What could he be after? Is he looking for somebody – hoping to run across someone?'

Rogers sighed. 'Maybe he's trying to wear us out.' He opened the Martino dossier in front of him, turned to the proper page, and ran his finger down the scant list of names. 'Martino had exactly one relative in New York, and no close friends. There's this woman who sent him the wedding announcement. He seems to have gone with her for a while, while he was at C.C.N.Y. Maybe that's a possibility.'

'You're saying this man might be Martino.'

'I'm saying no such thing. He hasn't made a move towards her place, and it's no more than five blocks outside the area he's been covering. If anything, I'm saying he's not Martino.'

'Would you want to visit an old girl friend that's been married fifteen years?'

'Maybe.'

'It doesn't prove anything one way or another.'

'I believe that's what we've been saying right along.'

Finchley's mouth quirked. His eyes were expressionless. 'What about that relative?'

'His uncle? Martino used to work in his coffee house, right down that area. The coffee house is a barber-shop now. The uncle married a widow when he was sixty-three, moved to California with her, and died ten years ago. So that cleans it up. Martino didn't make friends, and had no relatives. He wasn't a joiner, and he didn't keep a diary. If there was ever anyone made for this kind of thing, Martino's the one.' Rogers clawed at his scalp.

'And yet,' Finchley said, 'he came straight to New York, and straight down into the Village. He must have had a reason. But, whatever it was, all he's doing is walking. Around and around. In circles. It doesn't tie in. It doesn't make sense – not for a man of this calibre.' Finchley's voice was troubled, and Rogers, remembering the episode between them earlier in the afternoon, gave him a sharp look. Rogers was still ashamed of his part in it, and didn't care to have it revived.

He picked up his phone. 'I'll order some food sent up.'

2

The drugstore on the corner of Sixth Avenue and West Seventh Street was small, with one narrow, twisting space of clear floor between the crowded counters. Like all small druggists, the owner had been forced to nail uprights to the counters and put shelves between them. Even so, there was barely room to display everything he had to carry in competition with the chain store up the street.

Salesmen had piled their display racks on every inch of eye-level surface, and tacked their advertising cards wherever they could. There was only one overhead cluster of fluorescent tubes, and the tight space behind the counter was always dark. There was one break in the wall of merchandise on the counters. There, behind an opening walled by two stands of cosmetics and roofed by a razor-blade card, the druggist sat behind his cash register, reading a newspaper.

He looked up as he heard the door open and close. His eyes went immediately to the metal side of the display case across from him, which he used for a mirror. The case was scuffed, and a little dirty. The druggist saw the vague outline of a man's large silhouette, but the creaking of the floorboards had already told him as much. He peered for a look at the face, and brought one hand up to the temple bar of his glasses. He got out of his chair, still holding his paper in his other hand, and thrust his head and shoulders out over the counter.

'Something I can do for – '

The man who'd come in turned his glittering face towards him. 'Where's your telephone books, please?' he asked quietly.

The druggist had no idea of what he might have done in another minute. But the matter-of-fact words gave him an easy response. 'Back through there,' he said, pointing to a narrow opening between two counters.

'Thank you.' The man squeezed himself through, and the druggist heard him turning pages. There was a faint rustle as he pulled a sheet out of the telephone company's notepaper dispenser. The druggist heard him take out a pencil with a faint click of its clip. Then the telephone book thudded back into its slot, and the man came out, folding the note and putting it in his breast pocket. 'Thank you very much,' he said. 'Good night.'

'Good night,' the druggist answered.

The man left the store. The druggist sat back on his chair, folding the paper on his knee.

It was a peculiar thing, the druggist thought, looking blankly down at his paper. But the man hadn't seemed to be conscious of anything peculiar about himself. He hadn't offered any explanations; he hadn't done anything except ask a perfectly reasonable question. People came in here twenty times a day and asked the same thing.

So it couldn't really be anything worth getting excited about. Well – yes, of course it was, but the metal-headed man hadn't seemed to think so. And it would be his business, wouldn't it?

The druggist decided that it was something to think about, and to mention to his wife when he got home. But it wasn't anything to be panicked by.

In a very brief space of time, his eyes were automatically following print. Soon he was reading again. When Rogers' man came in a minute later, that was the way he found him.

Rogers' man was one of a team of two. His partner had stayed with their man, following him up the street.

He looked around the drugstore. 'Anybody here?'

The druggist's head and shoulders came into sight behind the counter. 'Yes, mister?'

The Security man fished in his pocket. 'Got a packet of Chesterfields?'

The druggist nodded and slipped the cigarettes out of the rack behind the counter. He picked up the half dollar the Security man put down.

'Say,' the Security man said with a puzzled frown, 'did I just see a guy wearing a tin mask walk out of here?'

The druggist nodded. 'That's right. It didn't seem to be a mask, though.'

'I'll be damned. I *thought* I saw this fellow, but it's kind of a hard thing to believe.'

'That's what happened.'

The Security man shook his head. 'Well, I guess you see all kinds of people in this part of town. You figure he was dressed up to advertise a play, or something?'

'Don't ask me. He wasn't carrying a sign or anything.'

'What'd he do – buy a can of metal polish?' The Security man grinned.

'Just looked in a phone book, that's all. Didn't even make a call.' The druggist scratched his head. 'I guess he was just looking up an address.'

'Boy, I wonder who *he's* visiting! Well' – and he shrugged – 'you sure do run into some funny people down here.'

'Oh, I don't know,' the druggist said a little testily, 'I've seen some crazy-looking things in other parts of town, too.'

'Yeah, sure. I guess so. Say – speakin' of phones, I guess I might as well call this girl. Where's it at?'

'Back there,' the druggist said, pointing.

'O.K., thanks.' The Security man pushed through the space between the two counters. He stood looking sourly down at the stand of phone books. He pulled the top sheet out of the note dispenser, looked at it for impressions, and saw none that made any sense. He slipped the paper into his pocket, looked at the books again – six of them, counting the Manhattan Classified – and shook his head. Then he stepped into the booth, dropped coins into the slot, and dialled Rogers' office.

3

The clock on Rogers' desk read a few minutes past nine. Rogers still sat behind his desk, and Finchley waited in the chair beside it.

Rogers felt tired. He'd been up some twenty-two hours, and the fact that Finchley and their man had done the same was no help.

It's piled up on me, he thought. Day after day without enough sleep, and tension all the time. I should have been in bed hours ago.

But Finchley had gone through it all with him. And their man must feel infinitely worse. And what was a little lost sleep compared to what the man had lost? Still Rogers was feeling sick to his stomach. His eyes were burning. His scalp was numb with exhaustion, and he had a vile taste in his mouth. He wondered if sticking to the job was made any the less because Finchley was younger and could take it, or because the metal-faced man was still following his ghost up and down the city streets. He decided it was.

'I hate to ask you to stay here so late, Finch,' he said.

Finchley shrugged. 'That's the job, isn't it?' He picked up the piece of Danish pastry left over from supper, swirled his cold half-container of coffee, and took a swallow. 'I've got to admit I hope this doesn't happen every night. But I can't understand what he's doing.'

Rogers toyed with the blotter on his desk, pushing it back and forth with his fingertips. 'We ought to be getting another report fairly soon. Maybe he's done something.'

'Maybe he's going to sleep in the park.'

'The city police'll pick him up if he tries to.'

'What about that? What's the procedure if he's arrested for a civil crime?'

'One more complication.' Rogers shook his head hopelessly, drugged by fatigue. 'I briefed the Commission's office, and we've got cooperation on the administrative level. It'd be a poor move to issue a general order for all patrolmen to leave him alone. Somebody'd let it slip. The theory is that beat patrolmen will call in to their precinct houses if they spot a metalheaded man. The precinct captains have instructions that he's to be left alone. But if a patrolman arrests him for vagrancy before he calls in, then all kinds of things could go wrong. It'll be straightened out in a hurry, but it might get on record somewhere. Then, in a few years from now, somebody doing a book or something might come across the record, and that'll be that. We can't keep the publishers bottled up for ever.' Rogers sighed, 'I only hope it'd be a few years from now.' He looked down at his desktop. 'It's a mess. This world was never organized to include a faceless man.'

It's true, he thought. Just by being alive, he's made me stumble from the very start. Look at us all – Security, the whole A.N.G. – handcuffed because we couldn't simply shoot him and get him out of the way. Going around in circles, trying to find an answer. And he hasn't yet *done* anything.

For some reason, Rogers found himself thinking, 'Commit a crime and the world is made of glass.' Emerson. Rogers grunted.

The telephone rang.

He picked it up and listened.

'All right,' he said finally, 'get back to your partner. I'll have somebody intercept and pick that paper up from you. Call in when your man gets to wherever he's going.' He hung up. 'He's made a move,' he told Finchley. 'He looked up an address in a phone book.'

'Any idea of whose?'

'I'm not sure . . .' Rogers flipped the Martino dossier open.

'The girl,' Finchley said. 'The one he used to know.'

'Maybe. If he thinks they're still close enough for her to do him any good. Why did he have to look up the address? It's the same as the one on the wedding announcement.'

'It's been fifteen years, Shawn. He could have forgotten it.'

'He may never have known it.' And there was no guarantee the man was going to the address he'd copied. He might have looked it up for some future purpose. They couldn't take chances. Everything had to be covered. The phone books had to be examined. There might be some mark – some oily fingerprint, wet with perspiration, some pencil mark; some trace –

Six New York City phone books. God knew how many pages, each had to be checked.

'Finch, your people'll have to furnish a current set of New York phone books. Worn ones. We're going to switch 'em for a set I want run through your labs. Got to have 'em right away.'

Finchley nodded and reached for the phone.

4

A travel-worn young man, lugging a scuffed cardboard suitcase, came into the drugstore on the corner of Sixth Avenue and West Seventh Street.

'Like to make a phone call,' he said to the druggist. 'Where is it?'

The druggist told him, and the young man just managed to get his suitcase through the narrow gap between the counters. He bumped it about clumsily for a few moments, and shifted it back and forth, annoying the druggist at his cash register, while he made his call.

When he left, the druggist's original books went to the F.B.I. laboratory, where the top sheet of notepaper had already checked out useless.

The Manhattan book was run through first, on the assumption that it was the likeliest. The technicians did not work page by page. They had a book with all Manhattan phones listed by subscribers' addresses, and they laid out a square search pattern centring on the drugstore. An IBM machine arranged the nearest subscribers' addresses in alphabetical order, and then the technicians began to work on the book taken from the store, using their new list to skip whole columns of numbers that had a low probability under this system.

Rogers hadn't supplied the technicians with Edith Chester's name. It would have done no good. By the time the results came through, the man would have reached there. If that was where he was going. Furthermore, there was no proof he'd only looked up one address. Eventually, all six books would be checked out, and probably show nothing. But the check would be made, and no one knew how many others afterwards.

Commit a crime and the world is made of glass.

5

Edith Chester Hayes lived in the back apartment on the second floor of a house off Sullivan Street. The soot of eighty years had settled in every brick, and industrial fumes had gnawed the paint into flakes. A narrow doorway opened into the street, and a dim yellow bulb glowed in the foyer. Battered garbage cans stood in front of the ground floor windows.

Rogers looked out at it from his seat in an F.B.I. special car. 'You always expect them to have torn these places down,' he said.

'They do,' Finchley answered. 'But other houses grow old faster than these get condemned.' His voice was distracted as though he were thinking of something else, and thinking of it so intently that he barely heard what he was saying. He hunched in his corner of the back seat, his hand slowly rubbing the side of his face. He paid no attention when one of the A.N.G. team that had followed the man here came up to the car and leaned in Rogers' window.

'He's upstairs, on the second floor landing, Mr Rogers,' the man said. 'He's been there for fifteen minutes, ever since we got here. He hasn't knocked on any door. He's just up there, leaning against a wall.'

'Didn't he even ring a doorbell?' Rogers asked. 'How'd he get into the building?'

'They never lock the front doors in these places, Mr Rogers. Anybody can get into the halls any time they want to.'

'Well, how long can he stay up there? Some tenant's bound to come along and see him. That'll start a fuss. And what's the point of his just staying in the hall?'

'I couldn't say, Mr Rogers. Nothing he's done all day makes sense. But he's got to make a move pretty soon, even if it's just coming back down and starting this walking around business again.'

Rogers leaned over the front seat and tapped the shoulder of the F.B.I. technician, wearing headphones, who was bent over a small receiving set. 'What's going on?'

The technician slipped one phone. 'All I'm getting is breathing. And he's shuffing his feet once in a while.'

'Will you be able to follow him if he moves?'

'If he stays in a narrow hall, or stands near a wall in a room, yes, sir. These induction microphones're pretty sensitive, and I've got it flat against a riser halfway up the first floor stairs. I can move it in behind him, if he goes into an apartment.'

'Won't he see it?'

'Probably not unless it's in motion when he looks. And we can tell if anyone's facing towards it by the volume of the sounds they make. It looks like a matchbook, and it's got little sticky plastic treads it crawls on. It doesn't make any noise, and the wires it trails are only hairlines. We've never had any trouble with one of these gadgets.'

'I see. Let me know if he does anyth –'

'He's moving.' The technician snapped a switch, and Rogers heard the sound of heavy footsteps on the sagging hall floor boards. Then the man knocked softly on a door, his knuckles barely rapping the wood before he stopped.

'I'm going to get a little closer,' the technician said. They heard the microphone scrape quietly up the stairs. Then the speaker was full of the man's heavy breathing.

'What's he upset about?' Rogers wondered.

They heard the man knock hesitantly again. His feet moved nervously.

Someone was coming towards the door. They heard it open, and then heard a gasp of indrawn breath. There was no way of telling whether their man had made the sound or not.

'Yes?' It was a woman, taken by surprise.

'Edith?' The man's voice was low and abashed.

Finchley straightened out of his slump. 'That's it – that explains it. He spent all day working up his nerve.'

'Nerve for what? Proves nothing,' Rogers growled.

'I'm Edith Hayes,' the woman's voice said cautiously.

'Edith – I'm Luke. Lucas Martino.'

'Luke!'

'I was in an accident, Edith. I just left the hospital a few weeks ago. I've been retired.'

Rogers grunted. 'Got his story all straight, hasn't he?'

'He's had all day to think of how to put it,' Finchley said. 'What do you expect him to do? Tell her the history of twenty years while he stands in her doorway?'

'Maybe.'

'For Pete's sake, Shawn, if this isn't Martino how'd he know about her?'

'I can think of lots of ways Azarin could get this kind of detail out of a man.'

'It's not likely.'

'Nothing's likely. It's not likely any one particular germ cell would grow up to be Lucas Martino. I've got to remember Azarin's a thorough man.'

'Edith —' the man's voice said, 'may I come in for a moment?'

The woman hesitated for a second. Then she said, 'Yes, of course.'

The man sighed. 'Thank you.'

He stepped into the apartment and the door closed. The F.B.I. technician moved the microphone forward and jammed it tightly against the panels.

'Sit down, Luke.'

'Thank you.' They sat in silence for a few moments. 'You have a very nice-looking apartment, Edith. It's been fixed up very comfortably.'

'Sam — my husband — liked to work with his hands,' the woman said awkwardly. 'He did it. He spent a long time over it. He's dead now. He fell from a building he was working on.'

There was another pause. The man said, 'I'm sorry I was never able to come down and see you after I left college.'

'I think you and Sam would have liked each other. He was a good deal like you, orderly.'

'I didn't think I ever showed much of that with you.'

'I could see it.'

The man cleared his throat nervously. 'You're looking

very well Edith. Have you been getting along all right?'

'I'm fine. I work. Susan stays at a friend's house after school until I pick her up on my way home at night.'

'I didn't know you had children.'

'Susan's eleven. She's a very bright little girl. I'm quite proud of her.'

'Is she asleep now?'

'Oh, yes – it's well past her bedtime.'

'I'm sorry I came so late. I'll keep my voice down.'

'I wasn't hinting, Luke.'

' – I know. But it is late. I'll be going in a minute.'

'You don't have to rush. I never go to bed before midnight.'

'But I'm sure you have things to do – clothes to iron, Susan's lunch to pack.'

'That only takes a few minutes. Luke –' Now the woman seemed steadier. 'We were always so uncomfortable around each other. Let's not keep to that old habit.'

'I'm sorry. Edith. You're right. But – do you know, I couldn't even call you and ask if I could come to see you? I tried, and I found myself imagining you'd refuse to see me. I spent all day nerving myself to do this.' The man was still uncomfortable. And as far as anyone listening could tell, he hadn't yet taken off his coat.

'What's the matter, Luke?'

'It's complicated. When I was in their – in the – hospital, I spent a long time thinking about us. Not as lovers, you understand, but as people – as friends. We never knew each other at all, did we? At least, I never knew you. I was too wrapped up in what I was doing and wanted to do. I never paid any real attention to you. I thought of you as a problem, not as a person. And I think I'm here tonight to apologize for that.'

'Luke –' The woman's voice started and stopped. She moved in her creaking chair. 'Would you like a cup of coffee?'

'I know I'm embarrassing you, Edith. I would have liked to handle this more gracefully. But I don't have much time. And it's almost impossible to be graceful when I have to come here looking like this.'

'That's not important,' she said quickly. 'And it doesn't

matter what you look like, as long as I know it's you. *Would* you like some coffee?'

The man's voice was troubled. 'All right, Edith. Thank you. We can't seem to stop being strangers, somehow, can we?'

'What makes you say that – No. You're right. I'm trying very hard, but I can't even fool myself. I'll start the water boiling.' Her footsteps, quick and erratic, faded into the kitchen.

The man sighed, sitting by himself in the living-room.

'Well, *now* what do you think?' Finchley demanded. 'Does that sound like Secret Operative X-Eight hatching a plan to blow up Geneva?'

'It sounds like a high school boy,' Rogers answered.

'He's lived behind walls all his life. They all sound like this. They know enough to split the world open like a rotten orange, and they've been allowed to mature to the age of sixteen.'

'We aren't here to set up new rules for handling scientists. We're here to find out if this man's Lucas Martino.'

'And we've found out.'

'We've found out, maybe, that a clever man can take a few bits of specific information, add what he's learned about some kinds of people being a great deal alike, talk generalities, and fool a woman who hasn't seen the original in twenty years.'

'You sound like a man backing into the last ditch with a lost argument.'

'Never mind what *I* sound like.'

'Just what do you suppose he's doing this for, if he isn't Martino?'

'A place to stay. Someone to run errands for him while he stays under cover. A base of operations.'

'Jesus Christ, man, don't you *ever* give up?'

'Finch, I'm dealing with a man who's smarter than I am.'

'Maybe a man with deeper emotions, too.'

'You think so?'

'No. No – sorry, Shawn.'

The woman's footsteps came back from the kitchen. She seemed to have used the time to gather herself. Her voice was firmer when she spoke once more.

'Lucas, is this your first day in New York?'

'Yes.'

'And the first thing you thought of was to come here. Why?'

'I'm not sure,' the man said, sounding more as if he didn't want to answer her. 'I told you I thought a great deal about us. Perhaps it became an obsession with me. I don't know. I shouldn't have done it, I suppose.'

'Why not? I must be the only person you know in New York, by now. You've been badly hurt, and you want someone to talk to. Why shouldn't you have come here?'

'I don't know.' The man sounded helpless. 'They're going to investigate you now, you know. They'll scrape through your past to find out where I belong. I hope you won't feel bad about that – I wouldn't have done it if I thought they'd find something to hurt you. I thought about it. But that wouldn't have stopped me from coming. That didn't seem as important as something else.'

'As what, Lucas?'

'I don't know.'

'Were you afraid I'd hate you? For what? For the way you look?'

'No! I don't think that little of you. You haven't even stared at me, or asked sneaking questions. And I knew you wouldn't.'

'Then –' The woman's voice was gentle, and calm, as though nothing could shake her for long. 'Then, did you think I'd hate you because you broke my heart?'

The man didn't answer.

'I was in love with you,' the woman said. 'If you thought I was, you were right. And when nothing ever came of it, you hurt me.'

Down in the car, Rogers grimaced with discomfort. The F.B.I. technician turned his head briefly. 'Don't let this kind of stuff throw you, Mr Rogers,' he said. 'We hear it all the time. It bothered me when I started, too. But after a while you come to realize that people shouldn't be ashamed to have this kind of thing listened to. It's honest, isn't it? It's what people talk about all over the world. They're not ashamed when they say it to each other, so you shouldn't feel funny about listening.'

'All right,' Finchley said, 'then suppose we all shut up and listen.'

'That's O.K., Mr Finchley,' the technician said. 'It's all going down on tape. We can play it back as often as we want to.' He turned back to his instruments. 'Besides, the man hasn't answered her yet. He's still thinking it over.'

'I'm sorry, Edith.'

'You've already apologized once tonight, Lucas.' The woman's chair scraped as she stood up. 'I don't want to see you crawling. I don't want you to feel you have to. I don't hate you – I never did. I loved you. I had found somebody to come alive to. When I met Sam, I knew how.'

'If you feel that way, Edith, I'm very glad for you.'

Her voice had a rueful smile in it. 'I didn't always feel that way about it. But you can do a great deal of thinking in twenty years.'

'Yes, you can.'

'It's odd. When you play the past over and over in your head, you can begin to see things in it that you missed when you were living it. You come to realize that there were moments when one word said differently, or one thing done at just the right time, would have changed everything.'

'That's true.'

'Of course, you have to remind yourself that you might be seeing things that were never there. You might be manoeuvring your memories to bring them into line with what you'd want them to be. You can't be sure you're not just daydreaming.'

'I suppose so.'

'A memory can be that way. It can become a perfect thing. The people in it become the people you'd like best, and never grow old – never change, never live twenty years away from you that turn them into somebody you can't recognize. The people in a memory are always just as you want them, and you can always go back to them and start exactly where you stopped, except that now you know where the mistakes were, and what should have been done. No friend is as good as the friend in a memory. No love is quite as wonderful.'

'Yes.'

'The – the water's boiling in the kitchen. I'll bring the coffee.'

'All right.'

'You're still wearing your coat, Lucas.'

'I'll take it off.'

'I'll be right back.'

Rogers looked at Finchley. 'What do you suppose she's leading up to?'

Finchley shook his head.

The woman came back from the kitchen. There was a clink of cups. 'I remembered not to put any cream or sugar in yours, Lucas.'

The man hesitated. 'That's very good of you, Edith. But – As a matter of fact, I can't stand it black any more. I'm sorry.'

'For what? For changing? Here – let me take that in the kitchen and do it right.'

'Just a little cream, please, Edith. And two spoons of sugar.'

Finchley asked. 'What do we know about Martino's recent coffee-drinking habits?'

'They can be checked,' Rogers answered.

'We'll have to be sure and do that.'

The woman brought the man's coffee. 'I hope this is all right, Lucas.'

'It's very good. I – I hope it doesn't upset you to watch me drink.'

'Should it? I have no trouble remembering you, Luke.'

They sat quietly for a few moments. Then the woman asked, 'Are you feeling better now?'

'Better?'

'You hadn't relaxed at all. You were as tense as you were that day you first spoke to me. In the zoo.'

'I can't help it, Edith.'

'I know. You came here hoping for something, but you can't even put it in words to yourself. You were always that way, Luke.'

'I've come to realize that,' the man said with a strained chuckle.

'Does laughing at it help you any, Luke?'

His voice fell again. 'I'm not sure.'

'Luke, if you want to go back to where we stopped, and begin it again, it's all right with me.'

'Edith?'

'If you want to court me.'

92

The man was deathly quiet for a moment. Then he heaved to his feet with a twang of the chair springs. 'Edith *look* at me. Think of the men that'll follow you and me until I die. And I am going to die. Not soon, but you'd be alone again just when people depend on each other most. I can't work. I couldn't even ask you to go anywhere with me. I can't do that, Edith. That's not what I came here for.'

'Isn't it what you thought of when you were lying in the hospital? Didn't you think of all these things against it, and still hope?'

'Edith –'

'Nothing could ever have come of it, the first time. And I loved Sam when I met him, and was happy to be his wife. But it's a different time, now and I've been remembering, too.'

In the car, Finchley muttered softly and with savage intensity, 'Don't mess it up, man. Don't foul it up. Do it right. Take your chance.' Then he realized Rogers was looking at him and he went abruptly quiet.

In the apartment, all the man's tension exploded out of his throat. 'I *can't* do it!'

'You can if I want you to,' the woman said gently.

The man sighed for one last time, and Rogers could see him in his mind's eye – the straight, set shoulders loosening a little, the fingers uncurling; the man standing there and opening the clenched fist of himself. Martino or not, traitor or spy, the man had won – or found – a haven.

A door opened inside the apartment. A child's voice said sleepily, 'Mommy – I woke up. I heard a man talking. *Mommy – what's that?*'

The woman caught her breath. 'This is Luke, Susan,' she said quickly. 'He's an old friend of mine, and he just came back to town. I was going to tell you about him in the morning.' She crossed the room and her voice was lower, as if she was holding the child and speaking softly. But she was still talking very rapidly. 'Lucas is a very nice man, honey. He's been in an accident – a very bad accident – and the doctor had to do that to cure him. But it's not anything important.'

'He's just standing there, Mommy. He's *looking* at me!'

The man made a sound in his throat.

'Don't be afraid of me, Susan – I won't hurt you. Really, I won't.' The floor thudded to his weight as he moved clumsily towards the child. 'See? I'm really a very funny man. Look at me blink my eyes. See all the colours they turn? Aren't they funny?' He was breathing loudly. It was a continuous, unearthly noise in the microphone. 'Now, you're not afraid of me, are you?'

'Yes! Yes, I am. Get away from me! Mommy, Mommy, don't let him!'

'But he's a nice man, Susan. He wants to be your friend.'

'I can do other tricks, Susan. See? See my hand spin? Isn't that a funny trick? See me close my eyes?' The man's voice was urgent, now, and trembling under the nervous joviality.

'I don't like you! I don't like you! If you're a nice man, why don't you smile?'

They heard the man step back.

The woman said clumsily, 'He's smiling inside, honey,' but the man was saying 'I'd – I'd better go, Edith. I'll only upset her more if I stay.'

'Please – Luke –'

'I'll come back some other time. I'll call you.' He fumbled at the door latches.

'Luke – oh, here's your coat – Luke, I'll talk to her. I'll explain. She just woke up – she may have been having a nightmare. . . .' Her voice trailed away.

'Yes.' He opened the door, and the F.B.I. technician barely remembered to pull his microphone away.

'You *will* come back?'

'Of course, Edith.' He hesitated. 'I'll be in touch with you.'

'Luke –'

The man was on the stairs, coming down quickly. The crash of his footsteps was loud, then fading as he passed the microphone blindly. Rogers signalled frantically from the car, and the two waiting A.N.G. men began walking briskly in opposite directions away from the building. The man came out, tugging his hat on to his head. As he walked, his footsteps quickened. He turned up his coat collar. He was almost running. He passed one of the A.N.G. men, and the other cut quickly around a corner, circling the block to fall in with his partner.

The man disappeared into the night, with the surveillance team trying to keep up behind him.

The microphone, left on the stairs, was still listening.

'Mommy – Mommy – who's Lucas?'

The woman's voice was very low. 'It doesn't matter, honey. Not any more.'

6

'All right,' Rogers said harshly, 'let's get going before he gets away from us.' He braced himself as the technician yanked his microphone back on its spring reel, thumbed the starter, and lurched the car forward.

Rogers was busy on his own radio, dispatching cover teams to cross the man's path and pick up the surveillance before he could outwalk the team behind him. Finchley had nothing to say as the car moved up the street. His face, as they passed under a light, was haggard.

The car rolled past the nearest A.N.G. man. He looked upset trying to walk fast enough to keep the hurrying man in sight and still not walk so fast as to attract attention. He threw a quick glance towards the car. His mouth was set, and his nostrils were flared.

Their headlights touched the bulky figure of their man. He was taking short, quick steps, his shoulders hunched and his hands in his pockets. He kept his face down.

'Where's he going now?' Rogers said unnecessarily. He didn't need Finchley to tell him.

'I don't think he knows,' Finchley said.

In the darkness, the man was walking uptown on MacDougal Street. The lights of the coffee shops above Bleecker lay waiting for him. He saw them and turned abruptly towards an alley.

A girl had come down the steps of the house beside him, and he brushed by her. He stopped, suddenly, and turned. He raised his head, his mouth falling open. He was frozen in a pantomime of surprise. He said something. The car lights splashed against his face.

The girl screamed. Her throat opened and she clapped her

hands to her eyes. The hideous sound she made was trapped in the narrow street.

The man began to run. He swerved into the alley, and even in the car, the sound of his feet was like someone pounding on a hollow box. The girl stood quiet now, bent forward, holding herself as though she were embarrassed.

'Get after him!' Rogers, in turn, was startled by the note his voice had struck. He dug his hands into the back of the front seat as the driver yanked the car into the alley.

The man was running well ahead of them. Their headlights shone on the back of his neck, and the glare of reflected light winked in the rippling shadows thrown by the flapping skirt of his trailing coat. He was running clumsily, like an exhausted man, and yet he was moving at fantastic speed.

'My God!' Finchley said. 'Look at him!'

'No human being can run like that,' Rogers said. 'He doesn't have to drive his lungs. He won't feel oxygen starvation as much. He'll push himself as fast as his heart can stand.'

'Or faster.'

The man threw himself against a wall, breaking his momentum. He thrust himself away, down a cross street, headed back downtown.

'*Come* on!' Rogers barked at the driver. 'Goose this hack.'

They screamed around the corner. The man was still far ahead, running without looking back. The street was lined with loading platforms at the backs of warehouses. There were no house lights and street lamps only at the corners. A row of traffic lights stretched down towards Canal Street, changing from green to red in a pre-set rhythm that rippled along the length of the street in waves. The man careered down among them like something flapping, driven by a giant wind.

'Jesus, Jesus, Jesus!' Finchley muttered urgently, 'He'll kill himself.'

The driver jammed speed into the car, flinging them over the truck-broken street. The man was already well past the next corner. Now he turned his head back for an instant and he saw them. He threw himself forward even faster, came to a cross street, and flailed around the corner, running towards Sixth Avenue now.

'That's a one-way street against us!' the driver yelled.

'Take it anyway, you idiot!' Finchley shouted back, and the car plunged west with the driver working frantically at the wheel. 'Now, *catch* him!' Finchley raged. 'We can't let him run to death!'

The street was lined with cars parked at the crowded kerbs. The clear space was just wide enough for a single car to squeeze through, and somewhere a few blocks ahead of them another set of headlights was coming towards them, growing closer.

The man was running desperately now. As the car began to catch him, Rogers could see his head turning from side to side, looking for some narrow alley-way between buildings, or some escape of any kind.

When they pulled even with him, Finchley cranked his window down. 'Martino! Stop! It's all right. Stop!'

The man turned his head, looked, and suddenly reversed his stride, squeezing between two parked cars with a rip of his coat and running across the street behind them.

The driver locked his brakes and threw the gear lever into reverse. The transmission broke up, but it held the driveshaft rigid. The car slid on motionless wheels, leaving a plume of smoke upon the street, the tyres bursting into flame. Rogers' face snapped forward into the seat back, and his teeth clicked together. Finchley tore his door open and jumped out.

'Martino!'

The man had reached the opposite sidewalk. Still running west, he did not stop or look behind. Finchley began to run along the street.

As Rogers cleared the doorway on his side, he saw the oncoming car just on the other side of the next street, no more than sixty feet away.

'Finch! Get off the street!'

Their man had reached the corner. Finchley was almost there, still in the street, not daring to waste time and fight his way between the bumper-to-bumper parked cars.

'Martino! Stop! You can't keep it up – Martino – you'll die!'

The oncoming car saw them and twisted frantically into the

cross street. But another car came around the corner from Mac-Dougal and caught Finchley with its pointed fender. It spun him violently away, his chest already crumpled, and threw him against the side of a parked car.

For one second, everything stopped. The car with the crushed fender stood rocking at the mouth of the street. Rogers kept one hand on the side of the F.B.I. car, the stench of burnt rubber swirling around him.

Then Rogers heard the man, far down a street, still running, and wondered if the man had really understood anything he'd heard since the girl screamed at him.

'Call in,' he snapped to the F.B.I. driver. 'Tell your headquarters to get in touch with my people. Tell them which way he's going, and to pick up the tail on him.' Then he ran across the street to Finchley, who was dead.

7

The hotel on Bleecker Street had a desk on the ground floor and narrow stairs going up to the rooms. The entrance was a narrow doorway between two stores. The clerk sat behind his desk, his chair tipped back against the stairs, and sleepily drooped his chin on his chest. He was an old, worn-out man with grey stubble on his face, and he was waiting for morning so he could go to bed.

The front door opened. The clerk did not look up. If somebody wanted a room, they'd come to him. When he heard the shuffling footsteps come to a stop in front of him, he opened his eyes.

The clerk was used to seeing cripples. The rooms upstairs were full of one kind or another. And the clerk was used to seeing new things all the time. When he was younger, he'd followed things in the paper. It had been no surprise to him when the Third Avenue El was torn down, or cars came out with four headlights. But now that he was older, things just drifted by him. So he never was surprised at anything he hadn't seen before. If doctors were putting metal heads on people, it wasn't much different from the aluminium artificial legs that often stumped up and down the stairs behind him.

The man in front of the desk was trying to talk to him. But for a long while, the only sound he made was a series of long, hollow, sucking sounds as air rushed into his mouth. He held on to the front edge of the desk for a moment. He touched the left side of his chest. Finally he said, labouring over the words, 'How much for a room?'

'Five bucks,' the clerk said, reaching behind him for a key. 'Cash in advance.'

The man fumbled with a wallet, took out a bill, and dropped it on the desk. He did not look directly at the clerk, and seemed to be trying to hide his face.

'Room number's on the key,' the clerk said, putting the money in the slot of a steel box bolted through the floor.

The man nodded quickly. 'All right.' He gestured self-consciously towards his face. 'I had an accident,' he said. 'An industrial accident. An explosion.'

'Buddy,' the clerk said, 'I don't give a damn. No drinking in your room and be out by eight o'clock, or it's another five bucks.'

8

It was almost nine o'clock in the morning. Rogers sat in his cold, blank office, listening to the telephone ring. After a time, he picked it up.

'Rogers.'

'This is Avery, sir. The subject is still in the hotel on Bleecker. He came down a little before eight, paid another day's rent, and went back to his room.'

'Thank you. Stay on it.'

He pushed the receiver back on the cradle and bent until his face was almost touching the desk. He clasped his hands behind his neck.

The inter-office buzzer made him straighten up again. He moved the switch over. 'Yes?'

'We have Miss DiFillipo here, sir.'

'Would you send her in, please.'

He waited until the girl came in, and then let his hand fall away from the switch. 'Come in, please. Here's – here's a chair for you.'

Angela DiFillipo was an attractive young brunette, a trifle on the thin side. Rogers judged her to be about eighteen. She came in confidently, and sat down without any trace of nervousness. Rogers imagined that in ordinary circumstances she was a calm, self-assured type, largely lacking in the little guilts that made even the most harmless people turn a bit nervous in this building.

'I'm Shawn Rogers,' he said, putting on a smile and holding out his hand.

She shook it firmly, almost mannishly, and smiled back without giving him the feeling that she was trying to make an impression on him. 'Hello.'

'I know you have to get to work, so I won't keep you here long.' He turned the recorder on. 'I'd just like to ask you a few questions about last night.'

'I'll be glad to help out.'

'Thank you. Now – your name is Angela DiFillipo, and you live at thirty-three MacDougal Street, here in New York, is that right?'

'Yes.'

'Last night – that would be the twelfth – at about ten-thirty p.m., you were at the corner of MacDougal and an alley between Bleecker and Houston Streets. Is that correct?'

'Yes.'

'Would you tell me how you got there and what happened?'

'Well, I'd just left the house to go to the delicatessen for some milk. The alley's right next to the door. I didn't particularly notice anybody, but I did know somebody was coming up MacDougal, because I could hear his footsteps.'

'Coming towards Bleecker? On the west side of the street?'

'Yes.'

'Go on, Miss DiFillipo. I may interrupt you again, to clarify the record, but you're doing fine.' And the record's piling up, he thought. For all the good it does.

'Well, I knew somebody was coming, but I didn't take any special notice of it, of course. I noticed he was walking fast. Then he changed direction, as if he was going to go into the alley. I looked at him then, because I wanted to get out of his way. There was a streetlight behind him, so all I could see was that it was a man – a big man – but I couldn't see his face. From the way he was walking, I didn't think he saw me at all. He was headed straight for me, though, and I guess I got a little tensed up.

'Anyhow, I took a short step back, and he just brushed my sleeve. That made him look up, and I saw there was something odd about his face.'

'How do you mean "odd," Miss DiFillipo?'

'Just odd. I didn't see what it was, then. But I got the feeling it had something wrong with it. And I guess that made me a little bit more nervous.'

'I see.'

'Then I saw his face. He stopped, and he opened his mouth – well, his face was metal, like one of those robot things in the Sunday paper, and it was where a mouth would be – and he looked surprised. And he said, in a very peculiar voice, "Barbara – it's I – the German." '

Rogers leaned forward in surprise. 'Barbara – it's I – the German? Are you sure of that?'

'Yes, sir. He sounded very surprised, and –'

'What is it, Miss DiFillipo?'

'I just realized what made me scream – I mean, what *really* did it.'

'Yes?'

'He said it in Italian.' She looked at Rogers with astonishment. 'I just realized that.'

Rogers frowned. 'He said it in Italian. And what he said was "Barbara – it's I – the German." That doesn't make sense, does it? Does it mean anything to you?'

The girl shook her head.

'Well.' Rogers looked down at the desk, where his hands were tapping a pencil on the blotter. 'How good is your Italian, Miss DiFillipo?'

'I speak it at home all the time.'

Rogers nodded. Then something else occurred to him. 'Tell me – I understand there are a number of regional Italian dialects. Could you tell which one he was using?'

'It sounded pretty usual. You might call it American Italian.'

'As if he'd been in the country a long time?'

'I guess so. He sounded pretty much like anybody around here. But I'm no expert. I just talk it.'

'I see. You don't know anyone named Barbara? I mean – a Barbara who looks a little like you, say?'

'No . . . no, I'm sure I don't.'

'All right, Miss DiFillipo. When he spoke to you, you screamed. Did anything else happen?'

'No. He turned around and ran into the alley. And then a car followed him in there. After that, one of your F.B.I. men came up to me and asked if I was all right. I told him I was, and he took me home. I guess you know all that.'

'Yes. And thank you, Miss DiFillipo. You've been very helpful. I don't think we'll need you again, but if we do we'll be in touch with you.'

'I'll be glad to help if I can, Mr Rogers. Good-bye.'

'Good-bye, Miss DiFillipo.' He shook her hand again, and watched her leave.

Damn, he thought, there's a kind of girl who wouldn't get upset if her man was in my kind of business.

Then he sat frowning. 'Barbara – it's I – the German.' Well, that was one more thing to check out.

He wondered how Martino was feeling, holed up in his room. And he wondered how soon – or how long – it would be before they came upon the kind of evidence you could put on record and have stand up.

The inter-office buzzer broke in on him again.

'Yes?'

'Mr Rogers? This is Reed. I've been running down some of the people on the Martino acquaintance list.'

'And?'

'This man, Francis Heywood, who was Lucas Martino's roommate at M.I.T.'

'The one who got to be a big gun in the A.N.G. Technical Personnel Allocations Bureau? He's dead. Died in a plane crash. What about him?'

'The F.B.I. just got a package on him. They pulled in a net of Soviet people in Washington. A really top-notch bunch, that'd been getting away with it for years. Sleepers, mostly.

When Heywood was in Washington for the American government, he was one of them.'

'The same Francis Heywood?'

'Fingerprints and photos check with our file, sir.'

Rogers let the air seep out between his lips. 'All right. Bring it here and let's have a look at it.' He hung up slowly.

When the F.B.I. file came in, the pattern it made was perfect, with no holes anyone couldn't fill with a little experienced conjecture, if he wanted to.

Francis Heywood had attended M.I.T. with Lucas Martino, sharing a room with him in one of the small dormitory apartments. Whether he was a Soviet sleeper even that far back was problematic. It made no significant difference. He was definitely one of them by the time he was transferred out of the American government into the A.N.G. Working for the A.N.G., he was hired to assign key technical personnel to the best working facilities for their specific purposes. He had been trained for this same kind of work in the American government, and was considered the best expert in the speciality. At some point near this period, he could have turned active. The natural conclusion was that he had been able to manoeuvre things so that the Soviets could get hold of Martino. Heywood, in effect, had been a talent scout.

He might, or might not, have known what K-Eighty-eight was. He was supposed to have only a rough idea of the projects he found space for, but it would certainly have been easier for him to make specific guesses than for most people. Or, if it was felt he ought to take the risk, he could have taken steps to find out. In any case, he had known what kind of man, and how important a project, he could deliver over the border.

That, again, was secondary. What mattered most was this:

A month after Lucas Martino had disappeared over the border, Francis Heywood had taken a transatlantic plane from Washington, where he had been on a liaison mission that might actually have been a cover for almost anything. The plane had reported engine explosions in mid-ocean, sent out a crash distress call, and fallen into the sea. Air rescue teams found some floating wreckage and recovered a few bodies, Francis

Heywood's not amongst them. The plane *had* crashed – sonar mapping found its pieces on the bottom. And, at the time, that had been that. Simple engine trouble of some kind. No report whatsoever of Soviet fighter planes sent out to create an incident, and the radio operator sending calm, well-trained messages to the last.

But now Rogers thought of the old business of dropping a man into the water at a prearranged spot, and having a submarine stand by to pick him up.

If you wanted to vary that so the man wouldn't be missed, then you could crash a whole commercial flight – who'd think it strange to miss one body? – and the submarine could make sure only that one man didn't drown. It was a little risky, but with the right kind of prearranged crash, and your man set for it, it was well within the kind of chance you took in this business.

He looked at Heywood's dossier statistics:

Height: 6 feet. Weight: 220. He'd been a heavy-set man, with a dark complexion. His age was almost exactly the same as Martino's. While in Europe, he had learnt to speak Italian – presumably with an American accent.

And Rogers wondered just how much Lucas Martino had told him, through three years in the same room. How much the lonely boy from New Jersey had talked about himself. Whether he might not have had a picture of his girl, Edith, on his desk. Or even of a girl called Barbara, for Heywood to have seen every day until it was completely soaked into his memory. Maybe Heywood could have explained what Angela DiFillipo had heard last night on MacDougal Street.

How good an actor was their man? Rogers wondered. How good an actor do you believe a man can be?

God help us, Finch, he thought.

Chapter 10

Young Lucas Martino came to Massachusetts Tech. convinced there was something wrong with him, determined to repair it if he could. But as he went through registration, drew his classroom assignments, and struggled to fit himself into a study routine like nothing he had ever met before, he began to realize how difficult that might be.

Tech. students were already handpicked on the day they entered. Tech. graduates were expected to fill positions at the top. A thousand projects were piled up on the Allied world's schedules, waiting for men to staff them. Once they were implemented, each project had a thousand other schedules waiting for completion. Plans made a dozen years ahead of time were ready, each timed, each meshed to another, each dependent on the successful completion of each schedule. If a man were some day to endanger that structure in any way, his weakness had to be located as early as possible.

So Tech. instructors were people who never gave a doubtful answer the benefit of the doubt. They did not drive their classes, or waste time in giving any particular student more attention than the next. Tech. students were presumed capable of digesting as much of the text as was assigned to them, and of knowing exactly what it meant. The instructors lectured quietly, competently, and ruthlessly, never going back to review a point or, in tests, to shade a mark because an otherwise good student had slipped once.

Lucas admired it as the ideal system for its purpose. The facts were presented, and those who could not grasp them, use them, and fit themselves to the class's progress, had to be eliminated before they slowed everybody down. It was a natural approach for him, and he had a tendency to be mildly

105

incredulous when someone in the next chair turned to him helplessly, already far behind and with no hope of catching up. In the first few weeks of school, he established himself among his class-mates as a cold, unfriendly brain, who acted as if he were somehow better than the rest of them.

His instructors, in that first year, took no notice of him. It was the potential failures that they were paid to pay attention to.

Lucas thought no more of that than he had at C.C.N.Y., where his teachers had been something close to over enthusiastic. He plunged into the work, not so much attracted to it as to the discovery that he *could* work – that it was expected of him, that he was given every opportunity to do so, and that the school was organized for people who could think in terms of work and nothing else.

It was almost two months before he became accustomed to it enough to lose the first edge of his enthusiasm. Then he could settle down and develop a routine. Then he had time for other things.

But he found that he was isolated. Somehow – he could not quite decide how – he had no friends. When he tried to approach some of his classmates, he found that they either resented him or were too busy. He discovered that most of them took at least half again as long at their assignments as he did, and that none of them were as sure of themselves as he. He puzzled over that – these were *Tech.* students, after all – and learned that most people could be content to know what they were doing only eighty-five per cent of the time. But that did nothing to help him.

It only confused him more. He had expected, without question, that here at Tech. he would meet a different breed of people. And, as a matter of fact, he had. There were plenty of students who abandoned every other concern when they came here. They slept little, ate hurriedly, and did nothing but study. In classes, they took notes at incredible length, took them back to their rooms at night, and pored over them. Letters from home went unanswered, and side trips into town at night were completely out of the question. Their conversation was a series of discussions about their work, and if any of them had personal problems, these were buried and left to take care of them-

106

selves while the grind of study went remorselessly on.

But, Lucas discovered, this did not mean that any of them were either happy or outstandingly familiar with their subjects. It only meant that they were temporary monomaniacs.

He wondered, for a while, if he might not be one, too. But the idea didn't seem to fit the facts. So, once again, he was forced to the conclusion that he was a sort of freak – someone who had, somewhere, missed a step most people took so naturally that they never noticed it. He found himself deeply worried by it, at those odd moments when his mind would let him. Through most of the day, he was completely absorbed in work. But, at night, when he sat in his room with the day's notes completed and the assignments read, when the current project was completed and he closed his books, then he sat staring blankly at the wall behind his desk and wondered what to do about the botch he'd made of Lucas Martino.

The only progress he ever made was in that brief time when he almost literally discovered his room-mate.

Frank Heywood was the ideal person to share a small room with Lucas Martino. A quiet, calm type who never spoke except when it was absolutely necessary, he seemed to fit his movements about the room so that they never interfered with Lucas'. He used the room only to sleep and study in, slipping out whenever he had any free time. When Lucas thought about it, some weeks after the year began, he decided that Frank, like himself, had been too busy for friendship or anything more than enough politeness to let them live in peace. But, evidently, Frank also settled down and began to find a little leisure, because it was his room-mate, and not Lucas, who initiated the short friendship between them.

'You know,' Frank astonished him by saying one night, 'you are without doubt the big gun in this student body.'

Lucas looked over from his desk, where he had been sitting with his chin in his hands. 'Who me?'

'Yes, you.' Heywood's expression was completely serious. 'I mean it. The word around the campus is you're a grind. That's a lot of bushwah. I've watched you, and you don't hit the books half as hard as most of these monkeys. You don't have to. One look and it's in your head for keeps.'

'So?'

'So you've got brains.'

'Not many morons get into a school like this.'

'Morons?' Frank gestured scornfully. 'Hell, no! This place is the cradle of next generation's good old American know-how, the hope of the future, the repository of all our finest young technical minds. And most of them couldn't give you the square of plus one without scratching their behinds and thinking about for an hour? Why? Because they've been taught what book to look it up in, not how to use it. But not you.'

Lucas looked at him in amazement. For one thing, this was by far the longest thing Frank had ever said to him. For another, here was a completely new viewpoint – an attitude towards Tech. and everything it represented that he had never heard before, and never considered.

'How do you mean that?' he asked, curious to learn as much about it as he could.

'Like this: the way things are taught around here, the only way most people can get through is by memorizing what they're told. I've been talking to some of these jokers. I'll bet you I can find ten guys right on this floor who can repeat their text back word for word, right down to the last comma, and do it like somebody pulling a tapeworm up his throat hand over hand. I will also bet you that if it turns out, fifteen years from now, that some Commie typesetter deliberately fouled up the words in the text, Allied science is going to be shot to hell because nobody'll have initiative enough to figure out what should have been there. Particularly not those ten guys. They'd keep on forever designing missile control systems that tuned in WBZ, because that was the way the book said to do it.'

'I still don't follow you,' Lucas said, frowning.

'Look – these guys aren't morons. They're pretty damned bright, or they wouldn't be here. But the only way they've ever been taught to learn something is to memorize it. If you throw a lot of new stuff at them in a hurry, they'll still memorize it – but they haven't got time to *think*. They just stuff in words, and when it comes time to show what they know, they unroll a piece. Yard goods.

'I say that's a hell of a dangerous thing to have going on. I

108

say anybody with brains ought to realize what he's doing to himself and the whole Allied effort when he stuffs facts down indiscriminately. I say anybody who *did* realize it would want to do something about it. But these clucks aren't even bothered by it enough to wrinkle their foreheads. So, considering everything, I say they may have brains, but they don't have brains *enough*.

'Now, you I've watched. When I sit here looking at you doing up your notes, it's a pleasure. Here's a guy with a look on his face as if he's looking at a love letter, for Christ's sake, when he's reading an electronics text. Here's a guy who fills out project reports like a man building a good watch. Here's a guy that's chewing before he swallows – here's a guy who's doing something with what they give him. Here, when you come right down to it, is a guy this place was *really* set up to produce.'

Lucas raised his eyebrows. 'Me?'

'You. I get around. I guess I've taken a look at every bird on this campus. There's a few like you on the faculty, but none in the student body. A few come close, but nobody touches you. That's why I say out of all the students here, all four classes, you're the guy to watch. You're the guy who's going to be really big in his field. I don't give a damn if it's civil engineering or nuclear dynamics.'

'Electronic physics, I think.'

'O.K., electronic physics. My money's on the Commies to be really worried about you in a few years' time.'

Lucas blinked. He was completely overwhelmed. 'I'm the illegitimate son of Guglielmo Marconi,' he said in reply. 'You notice the similarity in names.' But he couldn't do more with that defence than to put a temporary stop to Heywood's trend of conversation. He had to think it over – think hard, to arrange all this new data in its proper order.

In the first place, here was the brand-new notion that a difference from other people was not necessarily bad. Then, there was the idea that somebody actually thought enough of him to observe his behaviour and analyse it. That was not something he expected from people other than his parents. And, of course, the second conclusion led to a third. If Frank Heywood was thinking along lines like these, and if he could see what other people couldn't, then Frank too, was a person different from most.

That could mean a great deal. It could mean that he and Frank could at least talk to each other. Certainly it meant that Frank, despite his disclaimer, was just as capable as he – perhaps more so, since Frank had seen it and he had not.

In many ways, Lucas found this an attractive train of thought. If he accepted any part of it, it automatically meant he also accepted the idea that he was some kind of genius. That in itself made him look at the whole hypothesis suspiciously. But he had very little or no real evidence to refute it. In fact, it was the kind of hypothesis that made it possible to reinterpret his whole life, and thus reinterpret every piece of evidence that might have stood against it.

For several more weeks, he went through a period of great emotional intoxication, convinced that he had finally come to understand himself. In those weeks, he and Frank talked about whatever interested Lucas at the moment, and carried on serious discussions long into the night. But the feeling of being two geniuses together was an essential part of it, and one night Lucas thought to ask Frank how he was doing at his studies.

'Me? I'm doing fine. Half a point over passing grade, steady as a chalkline.'

'*Half* a point?'

Heywood grinned. 'You go to your church and I'll go to mine. I'll get a sheepskin that says Massachusetts Institute of Technology on it, the same as yours.'

'Yes, but it's not the diploma –'

' – it's what you know? Sure, if you're planning to go on from there. I could, to be completely honest, give even you a run for the money when it comes to that. But why the hell should I? I'm not going to sweat my *caliones* off at Yucca Flat for the next forty years, draw my pension, and retire. U-huh. I'm going to take that B.S. from M.I.T. and make it my entrance ticket into some government bureau, where I'll spend the next forty years sitting behind a desk, freezing my *caliones* off in an air-conditioned office, and some day I'll retire on a bigger pension.'

110

'And – and that's all?'

Heywood chuckled. 'That's all, *paisan*.'

'It sounds so God-damned empty I could spit. A guy with your brains, planning a life like that.'

Heywood grinned and spread his hands. 'There it is, though. So why should I kill myself here? This way I get by, and I've got lots of free time.' He grinned again. 'I get to have long talks with my room-mate, I get to run around and see other people – hell, amico, there's no sweat this way. And it takes a guy with brains to pull it in a grind house like Tech., I might add.'

It was the total waste of those brains that appalled Lucas. He found it impossible to understand and difficult to like. Certainly, it destroyed the mood of the past month.

He drew back into his shell after that. He was not hostile to Heywood, or anything like it, but he let the friendship die quickly. He lost, with it, any idea of being a genius. In time he even forgot that he had ever come close to making a fool of himself over it, though occasionally, when something went especially well for him in his later life, the idle thought would crop up to be instantly, and embarrassedly, suppressed.

He and Heywood finished their undergraduate work, still room-mates. Heywood was once more the perfect person for one small room with Lucas Martino, and seemed not to mind Lucas' long periods of complete silence. Sometimes Lucas saw him sitting and watching him.

After they graduated, Heywood left Boston and, as far as Lucas was concerned, disappeared. And it was only some years later that one of his graduate instructors came to him and said, 'This hypothesis you were talking about, Martino – it might be worth your doing a paper on it.'

So Heywood missed the birth of the K-Eighty-eight completely, and Lucas Martino, for his part, once again had something to claim all his attention and keep him from thinking about the unanswered problems in his mind.

Chapter 11

Edmund Starke had become an old man, living alone in a rented four-roomed bungalow on the edge of Bridgetown. He had dried to leathery hardness, his muscles turning into strings beneath his brittle skin, his veins thick and blue. The hair was gone from the top of his skull, revealing the hollows and ridges in the bone. His glasses were thick, and clumsy in their cheap frames. His jaw was set, thrust forward past his upper teeth, and his eyes were habitually narrowed. Like most old men, he slept little, resting in short naps rather than for very long at any one time. He spent his waking hours reading technical journals and working on an elementary physics textbook which, he felt suspiciously, was turning out to resemble every elementary physics text written before it.

Today he was sitting in the front room, twisting the spine of a journal in his fingers and peering across the room at the opposite wall. He heard footsteps on the dark porch outside and waited for the sound of the bell. When it came, he got up in his night robe and slippers, walked slowly to the door and opened it.

A big man stood in the doorway, his face bandaged bulkily, the collar of his coat pulled up and his hat low over his eyes. The light from the room glittered blankly on dark glasses.

'Well?' Starke rasped in his high, dry-throated voice.

The man wagged his head indecisively. The bandages over his jaw parted once, showing a dark slit, before he said anything. When he did speak, his voice was indistinct. 'Professor Starke.'

'Mister Starke. What is it?'

'I . . . don't know if you remember me. I was one of your students. Class of sixty-six at Bridgetown High School. I'm Lucas Martino.'

'Yes, I remember you. Come in.' Starke moved aside and held the door, pushing it shut carefully behind the man, disgusted at having to be so careful of draughts. 'Sit down. No, that's my chair. Take the one opposite.'

The chief impression his visitor was giving was one of embarrassment. He sat down gingerly, unsure of himself, and opened his coat with clumsy, gloved fingers.

'Take off your hat.' Starke lowered himself back into his chair and peered at the man. 'Ashamed of yourself?'

The man pulled the hat off, dragging it slowly. His entire skull was bandaged, the white gauze running down under his collar. He gestured towards it. 'An accident. An industrial accident,' he mumbled.

'That's none of my concern. What can I do for you?'

'I – I don't know,' the man said in a shocked voice, as though his plans had extended only to Starke's front door and he had never thought, till now, of what to do after that.

'What did you expect? Did you think I'd be surprised to see you? Or see you all wrapped up like the invisible man? I'm not. I know all about you. A man named Rogers was here and said you were on your way.' Starke cocked his head. 'So now you're caught flatfooted. Well – think. What're you going to do now?'

'I was afraid Rogers would find out about you. Did he bother you?'

'Not a bit.'

'What did he tell you?'

'He told me you might not be who you say you are. He wanted my opinion.'

'Didn't he tell you not to let me know that?'

'He did. I told him I'd do this my way.'

'You haven't changed.'

'How would you know?'

The man sighed. 'Then you don't think I'm Lucas Martino?'

'I don't care. It's no longer important whether you used to be in my class or not. If you're here for help of any kind, you've wasted your time.'

'I see.' The man began putting his hat back on.

'You'll wait and hear my reasons.'

'What reasons?' the man asked with dull bitterness. 'You don't trust me. That's a good reason.'

'If that's what you think, you'd better listen.'

The man sank back. 'All right.' He seemed not to care. His emotional responses seemed to reach him slowly and indistinctly, as if travelling through cotton wool.

'What would you want me to do?' Starke rasped. 'Take you in here to live with me? How long would that last – a month or two, a year? You'd have a corpse on your hands, and you'd still have no place to go. I'm an old man, Martino or whoever you are, and you ought to have taken that into account if you were making plans.'

The man shook his head.

'And if that's not what you wanted, then you wanted me to help you with some kind of work. Rogers said it might be that. Was that it?'

The man raised his hands helplessly.

Starke nodded. 'What made you think I was qualified? What made you think I could work on something forty years advanced over what I was taught at school? What made you think I could have kept up with the new work in the field? I don't have access to classified publications. Where did you think we'd get the equipment? What did you think would pay for it and –'

'I have some money.'

' – what did you think you'd gain by it if you did think you could answer those objections? This nation is effectively at war, and wouldn't tolerate unauthorized work for a moment. Or weren't you planning to work on anything important? Were you planning to drop corks into mousetraps?'

The man sat dumbly, his hands trailing over his thighs.

'Think, man.'

The man raised his hands and dropped them. He hunched forward. 'I thought I was.'

'You weren't.' Starke closed the subject. 'Now – where're you going to go from here?'

The man shook his head. 'I don't know. You know, I had decided you were my last chance.'

'Don't your parents live near here? If you are Martino?'

'They're both dead.' The man looked up. 'They didn't live to be as old as you.'

'Don't hate me for that. I'm sorry they're dead. Life wasn't meant to be given up gladly.'

'They left me the farm.'

'All right, then you've got a place to stay. Do you have a car?'

'No. I took the train down.'

'Muffled in your winding sheet, eh? Well, if you don't want to sleep in the hotel, take my car. It's in the garage. You can return it tomorrow. That'll get you there. The keys are on the mantelpiece.'

'Thank you.'

'Return the car, but don't visit me again. Lucas Martino was the one student whose brains I admired.'

2

'So you're not sure,' Rogers said heavily, sitting in the chair where the man had sat the night before.

'No.'

'Can you take an educated guess?'

'I think in facts. It's not a fact that he recognized me. He might have been bluffing. I saw no purpose in laying little traps for him, so I answered to my name. My picture has appeared in the local newspaper several times. 'Local Educator Retires After Long Service' was the most recent caption. He had my name to begin with. Am I to judge him incapable of elementary research?'

'He didn't visit the newspaper office, Mr Starke.'

'Mr Rogers, police work is your occupation, not mine. But if this man is a Soviet agent, he could easily have had the way prepared for him.'

'That's occurred to us, Mr Starke. We've found no conclusive proof of anything like that.'

'Lack of contrary proof does not establish the existence of a fact. Mr Rogers, you sound like a man trying to push someone into a decision you want.'

Rogers rubbed his hand along the back of his neck. 'All right, Mr Starke. Thank you very much for your cooperation.'

'I was a good deal more satisfied with my life before you and this man came into it.'

Rogers sighed. 'There's nothing very much any of us could do about that, is there?'

He left, made sure his surveillance teams were properly located, and went back to New York, driving up the turnpike at a slow and cautious rate.

3

Matteo Martino's old farm had stood abandoned for eight years. The fences were down, and the fields overgrown. The barn had lost its doors long ago, and all the windows of the house were broken. There was no paint left on the barn, and very little on the house. What there was, was cracked, peeling and useless. The inside of the house was littered, water-soaked, and filthy. Children had broken in often, despite the county police patrol, and scrawled messages on the walls. Someone had stolen the sinks, and someone else had hacked the few pieces of furniture left in it with a knife, at random.

The ground was ditched by gullies and flooded with rain-washed sand. Weeds had spread their tough roots into the soil. Someone had begun a trash pile along the remains of the back fence. The apple trees along the road were gnarled and grown out, their branches broken.

The first thing the man did was to have a telephone installed. He began ordering supplies from Bridgetown: food, clothes – overalls and work shirts, and heavy shoes – and then tools. No one questioned the legality of what he was doing – only Rogers could have raised the issue at all.

The surveillance teams watched him work. They saw him get up before dawn each morning, cook his meal in the improvised kitchen, and go out with his hammer and saw and nails while it was still too dark for anyone else to see what he was doing. They watched him drive fence posts and uncoil wire, tearing the weeds aside. They watched him set new beams into the barn, working alone, working slowly at first, and then more and more insistently, until the sound of the hammer never seemed to stop throughout the day.

He burned the old furniture and the old linoleum from the house. He ordered a bed, a kitchen table, and a chair, put them in the house, and did nothing more with it except gradually to set new panes in the windows as he found spare moments from re-shingling the barn. When that was done, he bought a tractor and a plough. He began to clear the land again.

He never left the farm. He spoke to none of the neighbours who tried to satisfy their curiosity. He did no trading at the general store. When the delivery trucks from Bridgetown filled his telephone orders, he gave unloading instructions with his order and never came out of the house while the trucks were in the yard.

Chapter 12

Lucas Martino stood looking up at the overhead maze of bus bars that fed power to the K-Eighty-eight. Down in the pit below his catwalk, he heard his technicians working around the thick, spherical, alloy tank, one of them cursed peevishly as he snagged his overalls on a protruding bolt head. The tank bristled with them. The production models would no doubt be streamlined and neatly painted, but here in this experimental installation, no one had seen any necessity for superfluous finishing. Except perhaps that technician.

As he watched, the technicians climbed out of the pit. The telephone rang beside him, and when he answered it the pit crew supervisor told him the tank area was cleared.

'All right. Thank you, Will. I'm starting the coolant pumps now.'

The outside of the tank began to frost. Martino dialled the power gang foreman. 'Ready for test, Allan.'

'I'll wind 'em up,' the foreman answered. 'You'll have full power any time you want it after thirty seconds from ... now. Good luck, Doctor Martino.'

'Thank you, Allan.'

He put the phone down and stood looking at the old brick wall across the enormous room. Plenty of space here, he thought. Not the way it was back in the States, when I was working with the undersized configurations because Kroenn's equations showed I could. I knew he was wrong, somewhere, but I couldn't prove it – I ought to know more mathematics, damn it. I do, but who can keep up with Kroenn? I remember, he was raving angry at himself for weeks when he found his own mistake.

It happens. The best of us slip a cog now and then. Well, it took Kroenn to see Kroenn's mistake. . . . Well, here we go . . .

He picked up the public address microphone and thumbed the button. 'Test,' his voice rumbled through the building. He put the microphone down and started the tape recorder.

'Test Number One, experimental K-Eighty-eight configuration two.' He gave the date. 'Applying power at –' he looked at his watch 'twenty-one hundred hours, thirty-two minutes.' He threw the switch and leaned over the railing to look down into the pit. The tank exploded.

Chapter 13

It was, once again, a rainy summer in New York. Grey day followed grey day, and even when the sun was out, the clouds waited at the edge of the horizon. The weather seemed to have gone bad all over the world. Hot winds scoured the great mid-continental plains of the north, and below the equator there was snow, and thaw, and snow, and thaw again. The oceans were never still, and from one seaboard to another the waves cracked against breakwaters with the hard, incessant slapping of high velocity artillery. Icebergs prowled down out of the polar caps, and migratory birds flew closer to the land. There were riots in Asia, and violent homicides in London.

Shawn Rogers left New York on a teeming day, the tyres of his car singing on wet blacktop, and for all his windscreen cleaner could do, the world seemed blurred, shifting, and impermanent. His car whined almost alone down the freeway, swaying in sharp lurches as the gusty wind struck it, and all the way down into the end of New Jersey the rain pursued him.

The secondary road to the farm surprised him by being wide, well graded, and smoothly surfaced. He was able to drive with only half his attention.

Five years, he thought, since I saw him last. Almost five since that night he came over the line. I wonder how he feels about things?

Rogers had his folders of daily reports, for the surveillance team still followed the man faithfully. A.N.G. men delivered his milk, A.N.G. men brought his rolls of fencing, and A.N.G. men sweated in the fields across from his farm. And every month, Rogers' secretary brought him a neatly typed résumé of everything the man did. But even though he always read them,

Rogers had learned how little was ever accurately abstracted from a man and successfully transferred to paper.

Rogers moved his mouth into a strained smile, his face tired and growing old. But what else was anyone to go by?

I wonder how he'll take the news I'm bringing?

Rogers swung the car around the curve, and saw the farm the surveillance team had so often photographed for him.

Set in one corner of the farm, the house was a freshly painted white building with green shutters. There was a lawn, carefully mowed and bordered by hedges, and across the yard from the house stood a solidly built barn, with a pickup truck parked in front of it, with no name lettered on its doors. There was a kitchen garden beside the house, laid out with geometrical exactness, the earth black, freshly weeded, and without a stone, textured like chocolate cream. A row of apple trees marched beside the road, every limb pruned, the foliage glistening with spray. The fence beside them shone with new wire, each post set exactly upright, every strand stretched perfectly parallel to the others. The fields lay green in the rain, furrows deep to carry off the excess water, and at the far end of the property, shrubs marked the edge of a small brook. As Rogers drove into the yard and stopped, a dog trotted out from behind the barn and stood in the rain, barking at him.

Rogers buttoned his raincoat and turned his collar up. He jumped out of the car, giving the door a hasty push shut, and ran across the yard to the back porch. As he reached its shelter, the door directly in front of him opened, and he found himself standing less than a foot away from the overalled man in the doorway.

There was change visible in the face. The metal had acquired a patina of microscopic scratches and scuffs, softening its machine-turned lustre and fogging the sharpness with which it reflected light. The eyes were the same, but the voice was different. It was duller, drier, and seemed to come out more slowly.

'Mr Rogers.'

'Hello, Mr Martino.'

'Come in.' The man stepped aside, out of the doorway. 'Thank you. I should have called first, but I wanted to be

121

sure we had a chance to talk at length.' Rogers stopped uncomfortably, just inside the door. 'There's something rather important to talk about, if you'll spare me the time . . .'

The man nodded. 'All right. I've got work to do, but you can come along and talk, I guess. I just cooked some lunch. There's enough for two.'

'Thank you.' Rogers took off his raincoat, and the man hung it up on a hook beside the kitchen door. 'I – how've you been?'

'All right. Chair over there. Sit down, and I'll get the food.' The man walked over to a cupboard and took down two plates.

Rogers sat down at the kitchen table, looking around stiffly for lack of something else to do.

The kitchen was neat and clean. There were curtains up over the sink, and there was fresh linoleum on the floor. There were no dishes left over on the drainboard, the sink itself had been scrubbed clean, and everything was put away carefully and systematically. Rogers tried to picture the man washing, ironing, and hanging curtains – doing it all according to a logically thought-out system, with not a move wasted, taking a minimum of time, as carefully as he'd ever set up a test series or checked the face of an oscilloscope. Day after day, for five years.

The man set a plate down in front of Rogers: boiled potatoes, beets, and a thick slice of pork tenderloin. 'Coffee? Just made some fresh.'

'Thanks. I'll take it black, please.'

'Suit yourself.' There was a faint grinding noise as the man put the cup down with his metal hand. Then he sat opposite Rogers and began to eat silently, without lifting his head or stopping. He was obviously impatient to get the necessary meal over and done with so he could get back to his work. Rogers had no choice but to eat as quickly as possible, and no opening to start talking. The meal was cooked well.

When they finished, the man stood up and silently gathered the plates and silverware, stacking them in the sink and running water over them. He handed Rogers a dish towel. 'I'd appreciate your drying these. We'll get done sooner.'

'Certainly.' They stood together at the sink, and as the man handed him each washed plate and cup, Rogers dried it carefully and put it in the drainboard rack. When they were through, the man put the dishes back in the cupboard, and Rogers started to put on his raincoat.

'Be with you in a minute,' the man said. He opened a drawer and took out a roll of bandaging. He held one end between the fingers of his metal hand and carefully wound a loose spiral up his arm, pushing his shirtsleeve out of the way. Taking safety pins out of his overall pocket, he fastened the two ends. Then he took a can of oil out of the drawer and carefully soaked the bandage before putting everything back and pushing the drawer shut. 'Got to do it,' he explained to Rogers. 'Dust and grit gets in there, and it wears.'

'Of course.'

'Well, let's go.'

Rogers followed the man out into the yard, and they walked across to the barn. The dog ran up beside them, and the man reached down to pat his neck. 'Get back in your house, stupe. You'll get wet. Go on, Prince. Go on, boy.' The dog sniffed uncertainly at Rogers, trotted along with them for a few steps, and turned back.

'Prince? Is that his name? Nice-looking dog. What breed is he?'

'Mongrel. He's got a barrel he sleeps in, back of the barn.'

'You don't keep him in the house, then?'

'He's a watchdog. He's got to be outside. And he's not housebroken.' The man looked at Rogers. 'A dog's a dog, you know. If the only friend a man had was a dog, it'd mean he couldn't get along with his own kind, wouldn't it?'

'I wouldn't exactly say that. You like the dog, don't you?'

'Yes.'

'Ashamed of it?'

'You're pushing again, Rogers.'

Rogers dropped his eyes. 'I suppose I was.'

They went into the barn, and the man switched on the lights. There was a tractor sitting in the middle of the barn, with a can full of drained transmission oil beside it. The man unrolled an oily tarpaulin, pulled it over beside the tractor, and laid out the tools that had been rolled inside it. 'I have to fix this transmission today,' he said. 'I bought this tractor second-hand, and the fellow that had it before chipped the gears. They've got to

be replaced today, because I've got a field to harrow tomorrow.'
He selected a wrench and slid under the tractor, on his back. He
began loosening the nuts around the rim of the gearbox
cover, paying no further attention to Rogers.

Rogers stood uncertainly beside the tractor, looking down at
the man working under it. Finally, he looked around for something to sit on. There was a box set against the barn wall, and
he went over, got it, and sat down beside the tractor, bending
forward until he could see the man's face. But that did him
little good. Even though the gearbox had been drained during
the morning, there was still oil dripping out of it. The man was
working by touch, his eyes and mouth tightly shuttered, deaf,
with dirty oil running in narrow streaks down across his skull.

Rogers sat and waited for ten minutes, watching the man's
hands working deftly at the cover, right hand guiding left, right
hand, with its wrench, breaking the nuts loose from their lugs,
then left hand taking the nuts off with its hard fingers. Finally,
the man put the wrench aside, locating the tool tarpaulin without difficulty, and lifted the cover down, dropping the nuts inside it. The left hand probed inside the gearbox, and a retaining
slide dropped out, into the waiting right hand. The slide, too,
went into the up-ended gearbox cover, and the left hand popped
the gears out of their mounts. The man wriggled out from
under the tractor and opened his eyes.

'I was going to ask you – '. Rogers began.

'Minute.' He stood up and took the worn gears over to a
work bench, where he held them up to the light, cursing bitterly. 'A man has no business buying machinery if he won't treat
it right. That's a damned good design, that transmission. No
reason in the world for anybody to have trouble with it.' His
voice was almost querulous. 'A machine won't ever let you
down, if you'll only take the trouble to use it right – use it the
way you're supposed to, for the jobs it's built to do. That's all.
All you have to do is understand it. And no machine's that
complicated an average man can't understand it. But nobody
tries. Nobody thinks a machine's worth understanding. What's
a machine after all? Just a few pieces of metal. One's exactly
like another, and you can always get another one just like it.

'But I'll tell you something, Mr Rogers – ' He turned sud-

124

denly, and faced across the barn. The light was behind him, and Rogers saw only his silhouette – the body lost in the shapeless, angular drape of the overalls, the shoulders square, and the head round and featureless. 'Even so, people don't like machines. Machines don't talk and tell you their troubles. Machines don't do anything but what they're made for. They sit there, doing their jobs, and one looks like another – but it may be breaking up inside. It may be getting ready to not plough your field, or not pump your water, or throw a piston into your lap. It might be getting ready to do *anything* – so people are afraid of them, a little bit, and won't take the trouble to understand them, and they treat them badly. So the machines break down more quickly, and people trust them less, and mistreat them more. So the manufacturers say, "What's the use of building good machines? The clucks'll only wreck 'em anyway," and build flimsy stuff, so there're very few good machines being made any more. And that's a shame.'

He dropped the gears on the bench and picked up a box holding the replacement set. Still angry, he ripped the top off the box, took out the gears, and brought them back to the tractor.

'Mr Martino – ' Rogers said again.

'Yes?' he asked, laying the gears out in sequence on the tarpaulin.

Now that he'd come to the point of saying it, Rogers didn't know how. He thought of the man, trapped in the casque of himself through these five years, and Rogers didn't know how to put it.

'Mr Martino, I'm here as the official representative of the Allied Nations Government, empowered to make you an offer.'

The man grunted, picking up the first gear and reaching up under the tractor to slip it in place.

'Frankly,' Rogers stumbled on, 'I don't think they quite knew how to say it, so they chose me to do it, thinking I knew you best.' He shrugged wryly. 'But I don't know you.'

'Nobody does,' the man said. 'What's the A.N.G. want?'

'Well, the point I was trying to make was that I probably won't phrase this properly. I don't want my fumbling to prejudice your decision.'

125

The man made an impatient sound. 'Get to it, man.' Then, with infinite gentleness, he slipped the gear into place and reached for the next.

'Well – you know things all over the world're getting tense again.'

'Yes.' He wriggled further under the tractor, reached over with his right hand, and helped his left locate the second gear exactly in place. 'What's that got to do with me?' He took the last gear, mounted it, and forced the tight retaining slide into position, moving the closely machined part only as firmly as needed and no more. He scooped the nuts out of the gearbox cover and began hand-tightening it back in place.

'Mr Martino – the A.N.G. has re-instituted the K-Eighty-eight programme. They'd like you to work on it.'

The man under the tractor reached for his wrench, and his fingers slipped on the oily metal. He twisted around and reached with his left arm. There was a faint click as his fingers closed over it firmly, and then he turned back and began taking up the gearbox lugs.

Rogers waited, and after a while the man said, 'So Besser failed.'

'I wouldn't know about that, Mr Martino.'

'He must have. I'm sorry for him – he really believed he was right. It's funny with scientists, you know – they're supposed to be objective and detached, and formulate theories according to the evidence. But a man's baby is a man's baby, and sometimes they feel it very badly when an idea of theirs is proved wrong.' He finished tightening the cover, and screwed the drain plug in firmly. He crawled out from under the tractor, put the wrench down, and carefully rolled up the tarpaulin. 'Well, that's done,' he said. He put the tarpaulin under his arm, bent to pick up the can full of old oil, and went over to the work bench, where he put the tools down and carefully poured the can out into a waste drum.

He took a new half-gallon can from a rack, punched a pouring spout into its top, and brought it back to the tractor, where he took off the filler cap and up-ended the can over the transmission. 'Now I can get that field done tomorrow. The ground's got to be loosened up, you know, or it'll get crusty and cake.'

'Aren't you going to say anything about whether you'll accept the offer or not?'

The man lifted the pouring spout of the filler and replaced the cap. He put the empty can down and climbed up into the driver's saddle, where he began going carefully through the gears, testing them for engagement and smoothness, without looking at Rogers until he was satisfied he'd done a good job. Then he turned his head. 'They decided I was Martino?'

'I think', Rogers said slowly, 'they simply needed someone very badly. They felt, I think, that even if you weren't Lucas Martino, you'd have been trained to replace him. It – seems to be very important to them to get the K-Eighty-eight programme working again as quickly as possible. They have plenty of competent technicians. But geniuses don't appear often.'

The man climbed down off the tractor, picked up the empty oil can, and took it over to the bench. His arm bandage was black with floor dust, and he pulled a five-gallon can out from under the bench, uncapped it, and began taking the bandage off. The sharp smell of petrol burned into Rogers' nostrils.

'I was wonderin' how they'd come to decide for sure. I can't see any way of doing it.' He dropped the bandage into the petrol. Plunging both arms into the can, he washed the bandage clean and hung it over a nail to dry.

'You'd be watched very closely, of course. And probably kept under guard.'

'I wouldn't mind. I don't mind your people being around here all of the time.' He took a tin cup out of the bottom of the petrol can and sluiced down his arm, twisting and turning it to make sure every working part was washed out thoroughly. He took a stiff, fine-bristled brush from a rack and began cleaning his arm with methodical care, following an obviously old routine. Rogers watched him, wondering, once again, just what kind of brain lived behind that mask and was neither angry, nor bitter, nor triumphant that they'd had to come to him at last. 'But I can't do it,' the man said. He picked up an oil can and began lubricating his arm.

'Why not?' Rogers thought he saw the man's composure wavering.

The man shrugged uncomfortably. 'I can't do that stuff any

more.' The bandage was dry, and he wrapped his arm again. He didn't meet Rogers' eyes.

'What're you ashamed of?' Rogers asked.

The man walked over to the tractor, as though he thought it was safer there.

'What's the matter, Martino?'

The man put his left arm over the tractor's hood and stood facing out through the open barn doors. 'It's a pretty good life, here. I work my land, get it in shape ; I fix up the place – I guess you know what it was like when I moved in. It's been a lot of work. A lot of rebuildin'. Ten more years and I'll have it right in the shape I want.'

'You'll be dead.'

'I know. I don't care. I don't think about it. The thing is – ' His hand beat lightly on the tractor's hood. 'The thing is, I'm working all the time. A farm – everything on a farm – is so close to the edge between growing and rotting. You work the land, you grow crops, and when you do that, you're robbing the land. You're going to fertilize and irrigate, and lime, and drain, but the land doesn't know that. It's got to get back what you took out of it. Your fenceposts rot, your building foundations crumble, the rain comes down and your paint peels, your crops get beaten down and start to rot – you've got to work hard, every day, all day, just to stay a little bit better than even. You get up in the morning, and you have to make up for what's happened during the night. You can't do anything else. You don't think about anything else. Now you want me to go work on the K-Eighty-eight again.' Suddenly, his hand beat down on the tractor, and the barn echoed to the clang of metal. His voice was agonized. 'I'm not a physicist. I'm a farmer. I can't *do* that stuff any more!'

Rogers took a slow breath. 'All right – I'll go back and tell them.'

The man was quiet again. 'What're you going to do after that? Your men going to keep watching me?'

Rogers nodded. 'It has to be that way. I'll see you to your grave. I'm sorry.'

The man shrugged. 'I'm used to it. I haven't got anything that people watching is going to hurt.'

No, Rogers thought, you're harmless now. And I'm watching you, so I'm useless. I wonder if I'll end up living on a farm down the road?

Or is it just that you don't dare take the chance of going on the K-Eighty-eight project? Did they risk it, after all, with somebody who couldn't fool us there?

Rogers' mouth twisted. Once more — once more and for the thousandth time, he'd raise the old, pointless question. Something bubbled through his blood, and he shivered slightly. I'll be an old man, he thought, and I'll always think I knew, but I'll never get an answer.

'Martino,' he blurted. '*Are* you Martino?'

The man moved his head, and the metal glowed with a dull nimbus under its film of oil. He said nothing for a moment, his head moving from side to side as though he were looking for something lost. Then he tightened his grip on the tractor, and his shoulders came back. For a moment his voice had depth in it, as though he remembered something difficult and prideful he had done in his youth. 'No.'

Chapter 14

Anastas Azarin lifted the glass of lukewarm tea, pressed the spoon out of the way with his index finger, and drank it down without stopping until the glass was empty. He thumped it down in a circle of old stains on the end of his desk, and the spoon rattled. His orderly came in from the outer office, took the glass, refilled it, and set it down on the desk in easy reach. Azarin nodded shortly. The orderly clicked his heels, about-faced, and left the room.

Azarin watched him go, his mouth hooking deeply at one corner in a grimace of amusement that wrinkled all his face before it died as abruptly as it came. During that short moment, he had been transformed – his face had been open, frank, and friendly. But when his features smoothed again, all trace of the peasant, Azarin, left them. It was possible to see what Azarin had taught himself to become during his years of rising through the system: impersonal, efficient, wooden.

He went back to reading the weekly sector situation report, his blunt, nicotine-stained forefinger following the words, his lips muttering inaudibly.

He knew they laughed at him for his old-fashioned samovar. But the orderly knew what would happen to him if the glass ever remained empty. He knew they joked about the way he read. But they knew what would happen to them if he found errors in their reports.

Anastas Azarin had never graduated from their academies. He had never scribbled on their blackboards or filled their copybooks. While they were polishing the seats of their school uniforms on classroom benches, he had been out with his father, hefting an axe, and dragging the great baulks of timber through the dark forest. While they took their civil service examinations, he was supervising labour gangs on the taiga. While they hunched over their desks, he was in Mandjuria, eating bad rice with the little brown men. While they sat at home with their wives, reading their newspapers and dreaming of promotion, he was in a dressing station, dying of typhus.

And now he had a desk of his own, and an office of his own, and a pink-cheeked, wide-eyed orderly who brought him tea and clicked his heels. It was not their joke – it was his. It was he who could laugh – not they. They were nothing, and he was sector commandant – Anastas Azarin, Colonel, S.I.B. Gospodin Polkovnik Azarin, if you please!

He bent over the reports, muttering. Nothing new. As usual, the Allieds kept their sector tight. There was this American scientist, Martino. What was he doing, in his laboratory?

The American Heywood, could not tell. From his post with the Allied Nations Government, Heywood had managed to arrange things so that Martino's laboratory was placed close to Azarin's sector. But that was the best he had been able to do. He had known Martino, knew Martino was engaged in something important that required a room with a twenty-foot ceiling and eight hundred square feet of floor space, and was called Project K-Eighty-eight.

Azarin scowled. It was all very well and good to have such faith in Martino's importance, but *what* was K-Eighty-eight? What good was an empty name? The American Heywood, was very glib with his data, but the fact was that there was no data. The A.N.G. internal security system was such that no one, even Heywood, could know much of what was going on. That in itself was quite normal – the Soviet system was the same. But the fact was that in the end it would not be some cloak-and-dagger secret agent, with his flabby white skin and his little cameras, who would deliver the K-Eighty-eight to them. It would be Azarin – simple Anastas Azarin, the peasant – who would pull this thing apart as a bear destroys a dead tree to find the honey.

Martino would have to be interrogated. There was no other method of doing it. But for all Novoya Moskva wasted its air on the telephone, there was no quick way of doing it. There was no getting people into Martino's laboratory. He had to be waited for. Men had to be ready at all times, prepared to pluck him from some dark street on the day he wandered too close to the line, if that lucky accident ever did occur. Then – one two, three, he would be here, he would be questioned, he would be released, all in a matter of a few days before the Allieds could do anything, and the Allieds would have lost the K-Eighty-eight. And that devil, the American Rogers, no matter how clever he was, would have been taught at last that Anastas Azarin was a better man. But until that time, everyone – Azarin, Novoya Moskva – everyone – would have to wait. All in good time, if ever.

The telephone on his desk began to ring. Azarin swept up the receiver. 'Polkovnik Azarin,' he growled.

'Gospodin Polkovnik –' It was one of his staff assistants. Azarin recognized the voice and fumbled for the name. He found it.

'Well, Yung?'

'There has been an explosion in the American scientist's laboratory.'

'Get men in there. Get the American.'

'They are already on their way. What shall we do next?'

'Next? Bring him here. No – one moment. An explosion, you say? Take him to the military hospital.'

'Yes, sir. I very much hope he is alive, because this, of course, is the opportunity we have been waiting for.'

'Is it? Go give your orders.'

Azarin dropped the receiver on its cradle. This was bad. This was the worst possible thing. If Martino was dead, or so badly damaged as to be useless for weeks, Novoya Moskva would become intolerable.

2

As soon as his car had come to a stop in front of the hospital, Azarin jumped out and climbed quickly up the steps. He marched through the main doors and strode into the lobby, where a doctor was waiting for him.

'Colonel Azarin?' the wiry little doctor asked, bowing slightly from the waist. 'I am Medical Doctor Kothu. You will forgive me – I do not speak your language fluently.'

'I do well enough in yours,' Azarin said pleasantly, anticipating the gratifying surprise on the little man's face. When it came, it made him even more well disposed towards the doctor. 'Now, then – where is the man?'

'This way, please.' Kothu bowed again and led the way to the elevator. A brief smile touched Azarin's face as he followed him. It always gave him pleasure when simple-looking Anastas Azarin proved to be as learned as anyone who had spent years in the universities. It was something to be proud of, too, that he had learned the language while burning leeches off his legs in a jungle swamp, instead of out of some professor's book.

'How badly is the man injured?' he asked Kothu as they stepped out into another hall.

'Very badly. He was dead for a few moments.'

Azarin jerked his head towards the doctor.

Kothu nodded with a certain pride of his own. 'He died in the ambulance. Fortunately, death is no longer permanent, under certain circumstances.' He led Azarin to a plate glass window set in the wall of a white-tiled room. Inside, still wearing the torn remnants of his clothes, incredibly bloodied, a man lay in the midst of a welter of apparatus.

'He is quite safe now,' Kothu explained. 'You see the auto-jector there, pumping his blood, and the artificial kidney that purifies it. On this side are the artificial lungs,' The machines were bunched together haphazardly, where they had quickly been brought from their usual positions against the walls. Doctors and nurses were clustered around them, carefully supervising their workings, and other doctors were busy on the man himself, clamping torn blood vessels and applying compression to his armless left shoulder. As Azarin watched, orderlies began shifting the machines into systematic order. The emergency was over. Things were assuming a routine. A nurse glanced at her watch, looked over at a rack where a bottle was draining of whole blood, and substituted a fresh one.

Azarin scowled to hide his nervousness. He was having a certain amount of difficulty in keeping his glance on the monstrous scene. A man, after all, was made with his insides decently hidden under his skin. To look at a man, you did not

133

see the slimy organs doing their revolting work of keeping him alive and real. To see a man like this, ripped open, with mysteriously knowledgeable, yes – frightening – men like this Kothu pushing and pulling at the moist things that stuffed the smooth and handsome skin . . .

Azarin risked a sidelong glance at the little brown doctor. Kothu could do these abominable things just as easily to him. Anastas Azarin could lie there like that, hideously exposed, with men like this Kothu desecrating him at their pleasure.

'That's very good,' Azarin barked, 'but he's useless to me. Or can he speak?'

Kothu shook his head. 'His head is crushed, and he has lost a number of his sensory organs. But this is only emergency equipment, such as you will find in any accident ward. Inside of two months, he'll be as good as new.'

'Two *months*?'

'Colonel Azarin, I ask you to look at what lies on that table and is barely a man.'

'Yes – yes, of course. I'm lucky to have him at all. He can't be moved, I suppose? To the great hospital in Novoya Moskva, for example?'

'It would kill him.'

Azarin nodded. Well, with every bad, some good. There would be no question, now, of Martino being taken away from him. It would be Anastas Azarin who did it – Anastas Azarin who tore the honey from the tree.

'Very well – do your best. And quickly.'

'Of course, Colonel.'

'If there is anything you need, come to me. I will give it to you.'

'Yes, sir. Thank you.'

'There's nothing to thank me for. I want this man. You will do your best work to see that I get him.'

'Yes, Colonel.' Medical Doctor Kothu bowed slightly from the waist. Azarin nodded and walked away, down the hall to the elevator, his booted feet thudding against the floor.

Downstairs, he found Yung just driving up with a squad of S.I.B. soldiers. Azarin gave detailed instructions for a guard, and ordered the hospital's accident floor to be sealed off. Already, he was busy thinking of ways this story might be spreading. The ambulance crew had to be kept quiet, the hospital personnel might talk, and even some of the patients here might have gathered an idea of what was going on. All these leaks had to be plugged. Azarin went back to his car, conscious of how complex his work was, how much ability a man needed to do it properly, and of how, inevitably, the American, Rogers, would sooner or later bring it all to nothing.

Five weeks went by. Five weeks during which Azarin was unable to accomplish anything, and of which Martino knew nothing.

3

Every time Martino tried to focus his eyes, something whirred very softly in his frontal sinuses. He tried to understand that, but he felt very weak and boneless, and the sensation was so disconcerting that he was awake for an hour before he could see.

For that hour he lay motionless, listening, and noticing that his ears, too, were not serving him properly. Sounds advanced and receded much too quickly; were suddenly here and then there. His face ached slightly as each new vibration struck his ears, almost as if it were resonating to the sounds he heard.

There was some kind of apparatus in his mouth. His tongue felt the hard sleekness of metal, and the slipperiness of plastic. A splint, he thought. My jaw's broken. He tried it, and it worked very well. It must be some kind of traction splint, he thought.

Whatever it was, it kept his teeth from meeting. When he closed his jaws, he felt only pressure and resistance, instead of the mesh and grind of teeth coming together.

The sheets felt hot and rough, and his chest was constricted. The bandaging felt lumpy across his back. His right shoulder was painful when he tried to move it, but it moved. He opened and closed the fingers of his right hand. Good. He tried his left arm. Nothing. Bad.

He lay quietly for a while, and at the end of it he had accepted the fact that his arm was gone. He was right-handed, after all, and if the arm was the only thing, he was lucky. He set about testing, elevating his hips cautiously, flexing his thighs and calves, curling his toes. No paralysis.

He had been lucky, and now he felt much better. He tried his eyes again, and though the whirring came and jarred him, he kept focus this time. He looked up and saw a blue ceiling, with a blue light burning in its centre. The light bothered him, and after a moment he realized he wasn't blinking, so he blinked deliberately. The ceiling and the light turned yellow.

There had been a peculiar shifting across his field of vision. He looked down towards his feet. Yellow sheets, yellowish-white bedstead, yellow walls with a brown strip from floor to shoulder height. He blinked again, and the room went dark. He looked up towards the ceiling and barely saw a faint glow where the light had been, as though he were looking through leaded glass.

He couldn't feel the texture of the pillow against the back of his neck. He couldn't smell the smell of a hospital. He blinked again and the room was clear. He looked from side to side, and at the edge of his vision, just barely in sight and very close to his eyes, he saw two incurving cuts in what seemed to be metal plating. It was as though his face were pressed up to the door slit of a solitary confinement cell. He inched his right hand up to touch his face.

4

Five weeks – of which Martino knew nothing and during which Azarin had been unable to accomplish anything.

Azarin held the telephone headpiece in one hand and opened the inlaid sandalwood box on his desk with the other. He selected a gold-tipped papyros and put the tip in one corner of his mouth where it would be out of the way. There was a perpetual matchbox on his desk, and he jerked at the protruding match. It came free, but the pull had been too uneven to draw a proper spark out of the flint in the box. The match wick failed to catch light, and he thrust the match back into the box, jerked it out again, and once more failed to get a light. He swept the matchbox off his desk and into the wastebasket, pulled open his desk drawer, found real matches, and lit the papyros. His lip curled tightly to hold the cigarette and let him talk at the same time.

'Yes, sir. I appreciate that the Allieds are putting great pressure on us for the return of this man.' The connexion from Novoya Moskva was thin, but he did not raise his voice. Instead, he tightened it, giving it a hard, mechanical quality, as though he were driving it over the wires by force of will. He cursed silently at the speed with which Rogers had located Martino. It was one thing, negotiating with the Allieds when it was possible to say there was no knowledge of such a man. It was quite another when they could reply with the name of a specific hospital. It meant time lost that might have been stolen, and they were short of time to begin with. But there had never been any hiding anything important from Rogers for very long.

Very well, then that was the way it was. Meanwhile, however, there were these telephone calls.

'The surgeons will not have completed their final operation until tomorrow, at the earliest. I shall not be able to interrogate the man for perhaps two days thereafter. Yes, sir. I suggest the delay is the surgeons' responsibility. They say we are lucky to have the man alive at all, and that everything they are doing is absolutely necessary. Martino's condition was more serious. Every one of the operations was extremely delicate, and I am informed that nervous tissue regenerates very slowly, even with the most modern methods. Yes, sir. In my opinion, Medical Doctor Kothu is highly skilled. I am confirmed in this by my file copy of his certification from your headquarters.'

Azarin was gambling a little there, he knew. Central Headquarters might decide to step in whether it had an ostensible reason or not. But he thought they would wait for a time. Their own staff had passed on Kothu and the rest of the medical team in the local hospital, since it was a military establishment. They would hesitate to belie themselves. And they knew Azarin was one of their best men. At Central Headquarters, they did not laugh at him. They knew his record.

No, he could afford to gamble with his superiors. It was a valuable thing to practise, for a man who would some day be among the superiors and was readying himself for it.

'Yes, sir. Two weeks more.' Azarin bit down on the end of the papyros, and the hollow filter tube of gilt-wrapped pasteboard crumpled. He began chewing it lightly, sucking the smoke in between his teeth. 'Yes, sir. I am aware of the already long delay. I will bear the international situation in mind.'

Good. They were going to let him go ahead. For a moment, Azarin was happy.

Then the edge of his mind nibbled at the fact that he still had no idea of where to begin in his interrogation – that not the first shred of the earliest groundwork had been done.

Azarin scowled. Preoccupied, he said, 'Good-bye, sir,' put the telephone down, and sat with his elbows on the desk, leaning forward, the papyros held between the thumb and forefinger of his right hand.

He was very good at his work, he knew. But he had never before encountered precisely these conditions. Neither had Novoya Moskva, and that was a help, but it was no help on the direct problem.

These temporary detentions were normally quite cut-and-dried. The man was diplomatically pumped of whatever he would yield in a short space of time. Usually, this was little. Occasionally, it was more. But always the man was returned as quickly as possible. Except in cases where it was desirable to stir the Allieds up, for some larger purpose, it was always best not to anoy them. The Allieds, upset by something like this, could go to quite extraordinary lengths of retaliation, and no one could tell what other strategies they might not cripple with their countermoves. Similarly, there were certain methods it was best not to use on their people. Returning a man in bad condition invariably made things difficult for months afterwards.

So, usually it was a day or two at most before a man was returned to the Allieds. There, Rogers would take a day or two in discovering how much Azarin had found out. And that was the sum of it. If, at times, Azarin learned something useful, Rogers neutralized it at once. In Azarin's opinion, the entire business was a pitiful waste of time and energy.

But now, with this Martino, what did he have? He had a man who had invented something called a K-Eighty-eight, a

138

man of high but undocumented reputation. Once more, Azarin cursed the circumstances of the times in which he lived. Once more he was angrily conscious of the fact that it was being left for the working professional – for Anastas Azarin – to clean up the work done by such fumbling amateurs as Heywood.

Azarin stared down at his desk in blank fury. And, of course, Novoya Moskva refused to act as though such a thing was basically its own fault. They simply pressed Azarin for the results. Was he not an intelligence officer, after all? What could possibly be so difficult? What could possibly have taken him five weeks?

It was always this way in dealing with clerks. They had books, after all. The books had taught them how things were done. So things were done as they had been done in 1914 and in 1941, when the books were written.

No one knew anything about this man, except that he'd invented something. They had no file on him except for his undergraduate period at the technical academy in Cambridge, Massachusetts. Cursing, Azarin wished that the S.I.B. had, in actuality, some of the super-ferrets with which it was credited by the kino studios – the daring and supernally intelligent operatives who somehow passed through concrete walls and into vaults stuffed with alphabetically arranged Allied secrets conveniently shapirographed in Cyrillic print. He would have enjoyed having one or two of these on his staff, knowing that any information they brought back was completely accurate, correctly interpreted, did not have to be confirmed by other operatives, was up to date, had not been planted, and, furthermore, that these operatives had not meanwhile been subverted by Rogers. Such people did occur, of course. They immediately became instructors and staff officers, because they were altogether too few.

So there he had been, this Martino, protected by the usual security safeguards common to both sides. Azarin had planned some day to add the K-Eighty-eight to the always incomplete and usually obsolescent jigsaw puzzle of information that was the best anyone could do. But he had not planned to have it happen like this.

Now he had him. He'd had him five useless weeks already.

He had him almost fatally injured, bedridden, the makings of a good *cause célèbre* if he wasn't back in Allied hands soon – a man who looked extremely valuable, though he might turn out not to be – a man who, therefore, ought to be returned as soon as possible and kept as long as possible, and with whom, peculiarly, neither thing could be done at once.

It was a situation which verged on the comic in some of its aspects.

Azarin finished his papyros and shredded it to bits in the ash-tray. It was all far from hopeless. He already had the rough outline of a plan, and he was acting on it. He would get results.

But Azarin knew Rogers was almost inhumanly clever. He knew Rogers must be fully aware of the situation here. And Azarin did not like the thought that Rogers must be laughing at him.

5

A nurse put her head in the door of Martino's room. He slowly lowered his hand back to his side. The nurse disappeared, and in a moment a man with a white smock and skullcap came in.

He was a wiry, curly-haired little man with olive skin, broad, chisel-shaped teeth, and a knobbly jaw, who smiled down cheerfully as he took Martino's pulse.

'I'm very glad to see you awake. My name is Kothu, I am a medical doctor, how do you feel?'

Martino moved his head from side to side.

'I see. There was no help for it, it had to be done. There was very little cranial structure remaining, the sensory organs were largely obliterated. Fortunately, the nature of the damage-inflicting agency was severe flashburns which did not expose your brain tissue to prolonged heat, and followed by a slow concussive shockwave crushing your cranium without splintering. Not pleasant to hear, I know, but of all possible damages the best. The arm, I am afraid, was severed by a metallic fragment. Would you speak, please?'

Martino looked up at him. He was still ashamed of the scream that had brought the nurse. He tried to picture what he must look like – to visualize the mechanisms that evidently were replacing so many of his organs – and he could not recall exactly how he had produced the scream. He tried to gather air in his lungs for the expected effort of speech, but there was only a rolling sensation under his ribs, as though a wheel or turbine impeller were spinning there.

'Effort is unnecessary,' Dr Kothu said. 'Simply speak.'

'I –' It felt no different in his throat. He had thought to find his words trembling through the vibrator of an artificial larynx. Instead, it was his old voice. But his rib cage did not sink over deflating lungs, and his diaphragm did not push out air. It was effortless, as speech in a dream can be, and he had the feeling he could babble on and on without stopping, for paragraphs, for days, for ever. 'I – One, two, three, four. One, two, three, four. Do, re, mi, fa, sol, la, te, do.'

'Thank you, that is very helpful. Tell me, do you see me clearly? As I step back and move about, do your eyes follow and focus easily?'

'Yes.' But the servomotors hummed in his face, and he wanted to reach up and massage the bridge of his nose.

'Very good. Well, do you know you have been here over a month?'

Martino shook his head. Wasn't anyone trying to get him back? Or did they think he was dead?

'It was necessary to keep you under sedation. You realize, I hope, the extent of the work we had to do?'

Martino moved his chest and shoulders. He felt clumsy and unbalanced, and somehow awkward inside, as though his chest were a bag that had been filled with stones.

'A great deal was done.' Dr Kothu seemed justifiably proud. 'I would say that Medical Doctor Verstoff did very well in substituting the prosthetic cranium. And of course, Medical Doctors Ho and Jansky were responsible for the connexion of the prosthetic sensory organs to the proper brain centres, as Medical Technicians Debrett, Fonten, and Wassil were for the renal and respiratory complexes. I, myself, am in charge, having the honour to have developed the method of nervous tissue regeneration.' His voice dropped a bit. 'You would do us the kindness, perhaps, to mention our names when you return to the other side? I do not know your name,' he added quickly, 'nor am I intended to know your origin, but, you see, there are certain things a medical professional can perceive. On our side, we give three smallpox inoculations on the right arm. In any case –' Kothu seemed definitely embarrassed now. 'What we have done here is quite new, and quite outstanding. And on our side, in these days, they do not publish such things.'

'I'll try.'

'Thank you. There are so many great things being done on our side, by so many people. And your side does not know. If you knew, your people would so much more quickly come to us.'

Martino said nothing. An uncomfortable moment dragged by, and then Dr Kothu said, 'We must get you ready. One thing remains to be done, and we will have accomplished our best. That is the arm.' He smiled as he had when he first came in. 'I will call the nurses, and they will prepare you. I shall see you again in the operating theatre, and when we are finished, you will be as good as new.'

'Thank you, Doctor.'

Kothu left, and the nurses came in. They were two women dressed in heavily starched, thick white uniforms with head-dresses that were banded tightly across their foreheads and draped back to their shoulders, completely covering their hair. Their faces were a little rough-skinned, but clear, and expressionless. Their lips were compressed, as they had been taught to keep them by the traditions of their nursing academies, and they wore no cosmetics. Because none of the standard cues common to women of the Allied cultures were present, it was impossible to guess at their ages and arrive at an accurate answer. They undressed him and washed him without speaking to each other or to him. They removed the pad from his left shoulder, painted the area with a coloured germicide, loosely taped a new sterile pad in place, and moved him to an operating cart which one of them brought into the room.

They worked with complete competence, wasting no motion and dividing the work perfectly; they were a team that had risen above the flesh and beyond all skills but their one, completely mastered own, who had so far advanced in the perfect practice of their art that it did not matter whether Martino was there or not.

Martino remained passively silent, watching them without getting in their way, and they handled him as though he were a practice mannequin.

6

Azarin strode down the corridor towards Martino's room, with Kothu chattering beside him.

'Yes, Colonel, although he is not yet really strong, it is only a matter now of sufficient rest. All the operations were a great success.'

'He can talk at length?'

'Not today, perhaps. It depends on the subject of discussion, of course. Too much strain would be bad.'

'That will be largely his choice. He is in here?'

'Yes, Colonel.' The little doctor opened the door wide, and Azarin marched through.

He stopped as though someone had sunk a bayonet in his belly. He stared at the unholy thing in the bed.

Martino was looking at him, with the sheets around his chest. Azarin could see the dark hole where his eyes were, lurking out from the metal. The good arm was under the covers. The left lay across his lap, like the claw of something from the Moon. The creature said nothing, did nothing. It lay in its bed and looked at him.

Azarin glared at Kothu. 'You did not tell me he would look like this.'

The doctor was thunderstruck. 'But, I did! I very carefully described the prosthetic appliances. I assured you they were perfectly functional – engineering marvels – if, regrettably, not especially cosmetic. You approved!'

'You did not tell me he would look like this,' Azarin growled. 'You will now introduce me.'

'Of course,' Doctor Kothu said nervously. He turned hastily towards Martino. 'Sir, this is Colonel Azarin. He has come to see about your condition.'

Azarin forced himself to go over to the bed. His face

crinkled into its smile. 'How do you do?' he said in English, holding out his hand.

The thing in the bed reached out its good hand. 'I'm feeling better, thank you,' it said neutrally. 'How do you do?' Its hand, at least, was human. Azarin gripped it warmly. 'I am well, thank you. Would you like to talk? Doctor Kothu, you will bring me a chair, please. I will sit here, and we will talk.' He waited for Kothu to place the chair. 'Thank you. You will go now. I will call you when I wish to leave.'

'Of course, Colonel. Good afternoon, sir,' Kothu said to the thing in the bed, and left.

'Now, Doctor of Science Martino, we will talk,' Azarin said pleasantly, settling himself in his chair. 'I have been waiting for you to recover. I hope I am not inconveniencing you, sir, but I understand there are things that have waited – records to be completed, forms to fill in, and the like.' He shook his head. 'Paperwork, sir. Always paperwork.'

'Of course,' Martino said. Azarin had difficulty fitting the perfectly normal voice to the ugly face. 'I suppose our people have been annoying your people to get me back, and that always means a great deal of writing back and forth, doesn't it?'

Here is a clever one, Azarin thought. Within the first minute, he was trying to find out if his people were pressing hard. Well, they were, God knew, they were, if Novoya Moskva's tone of voice meant anything.

'There is always paperwork,' he said, smiling. 'You understand, I am responsible for this sector, and my people wish reports.' So, now you may guess as much as you wish. 'Are you comfortable? I hope everything is as it should be. You understand that as colonel in command of this sector, I ordered that you be given the best of all medical attention.'

'Quite comfortable, thank you.'

'I am sure that you, as a Doctor of Science, must be even more impressed with the work than I, as a simple soldier.'

'My speciality is electronics, Colonel, not servomechanics.'

Ah. So now we are even.

Less than even, Azarin thought angrily, for Martino had yet to give any sign of being helpful. It did not matter, after all, how much Martino did not find out.

These first talks were seldom very productive in themselves. But they set the tone of everything that followed. It was now that Azarin had to decide what tactics to use against this man. It was now that the lines would be drawn, and Azarin measured against Martino.

But how could anyone see what this man thought when his face was the face of a metal beast – a carved thing, unmoving, with no sign of anything? No anger, no fear, no indecision – no weakness!

Azarin scowled. Still, in the end he would win. He would rip behind that mask, and secrets would come spilling out.

If there is time, he reminded himself. Six weeks, now. Six weeks. How far would the Allieds stretch their patience? How far would the Allieds let Novoya Moskva stretch theirs?

He almost glared at the man. It was his fault this incredible affair had ever taken place. 'Tell me, Doctor Martino,' he said, 'don't you wonder why you are here, in one of our hospitals?'

'I assume you got the jump on our rescue teams.'

It was becoming clear to Azarin that this Martino intended to leave him no openings. 'Yes,' he smiled, 'but would you not expect your Allied government to take better safety precautions? Should they not have had teams close by?'

'I'm afraid I never thought about it very much.'

So. The man refused to tell him whether the K-Eighty-eight was normally considered an explosion hazard or not.

'And what *have* you thought about, Doctor of Science?'

The figure in the bed shrugged. 'Nothing much. I'm waiting to get out of here. It's been quite a while, hasn't it? I don't imagine you'll be able to keep me very long.'

Now the thing was deliberately trying to get him angry. Azarin did not like being reminded of the wasted weeks. 'My dear Doctor of Science, you are free to go almost as soon as you wish.'

'Yes – exactly. Almost.'

So. The thing understood the situation perfectly, and would not yield – no more than its face could break out into fearful sweat.

Azarin realized his own palms were damp.

Abruptly, Azarin stood up. There was no good in pursuing

this further. The lines were clearly drawn, the purpose of the talk was accomplished, nothing more could be done, and it was becoming more than he could stand to remain any longer with this monster. 'I must go. We will talk again.' Azarin bowed. 'Good afternoon, Doctor of Science Martino.'

'Good afternoon, Colonel Azarin.'

Azarin pushed the chair back against the wall and strode out. 'I am finished for today,' he growled to the waiting Doctor Kothu, and went back to his office, where he sat drinking tea and frowning at the telephone.

7

Doctor Kothu came in, examined him, and left. Martino lay back in his bed, thinking.

Azarin was going to be bad, he thought, if he was given the chance to build up his temper over any period of time. He wondered how much longer the A.N.G. would take to get him out of this.

But Martino's greatest preoccupation, at the moment, was the K-Eighty-eight. He had already decided what unlikely combination of factors had produced the explosion. Now, as he had been doing for the past several hours, he worked towards a new means of absorbing the terrific heat wastage that the K-Eighty-eight developed.

He found his thoughts drifting away from it and towards what had happened to him. He raised his new arm and looked at it in fascination before he forced himself off the subject. He flung the arm down on the bed beside him, out of his field of vision, and felt the shock against the mattress.

How long am I going to stay in this place? he thought. Kothu had told him he could be getting out of bed soon. How much good is that going to do me if they keep me on this side of the line indefinitely?

He wondered how much the Soviets knew about the K-Eighty-eight. Probably just enough so they'd do their best to keep him and pump it out of him. If they hadn't known anything, they'd never have come after him. If they knew enough to use, again, they wouldn't have bothered.

146

He wondered how far the Soviets would go before they were ready to give up. You heard all kinds of stories. Probably the same stories the Soviets heard about the A.N.G.

He was frightened, he suddenly realized. Frightened by what had happened to him, by what Kothu had done to save him, by the thought of having the Soviets somehow get the K-Eighty-eight out of him, by the sudden feeling of complete helplessness that came over him.

He wondered if he might be a coward. It was something he had not considered since the age when he learned the difference between physical bravery and courage. The possibility that he might do something irrational out of simple fear was new to him.

He lay in the bed, searching his mind for evidence, pro or con.

8

It was two months now, and still Azarin did not even know whether the K-Eighty-eight was a bomb, a death ray, or a new means of sharpening bayonets.

He had had several totally unsatisfactory talks with that thing, Martino, who would not give in. It was all very polite, and it told him nothing. A man – any man – he could have fought. But a blank-faced nothing like some nightmare in the dark forests, that sat in its wheelchair looking like the gods they worshipped in jungle temples, that knew if it waited long enough Azarin would be beaten – that was more than could be tolerated.

Azarin remembered this morning's call from Novoya Moskva, and suddenly he crashed his fist down upon his desk.

Their best man. They knew he was their best man, they knew he was Anastas Azarin, and yet they talked to him like that! *Clerks* talked to him like *that*!

It was all because they wanted to give Martino back to the Allieds as quickly as they could. If they would give Azarin time, it would be another matter. If Martino did not have to be returned at all, if certain methods could be used, then something might really be done.

Azarin sat behind his desk, searching for the answer. Something must be thought of to satisfy Novoya Moskva – to delay things until, inevitably, a way was found to handle this Martino. But nothing would satisfy Central Headquarters unless they could in turn satisfy the Allieds. And the Allieds would be satisfied with nothing less than Martino.

Azarin's eyes opened wide. His thick eyebrows rose into perfect semicircles. Then he reached for his telephone and called Doctor Kothu's number. He sat listening to the telephone ring. He made one, Azarin thought. Perhaps he can make two.

His upper lip drew back from his teeth at the thought that the American Heywood, was the best choice for the assignment. He would have much preferred to send someone solid – one of his own people, whose capabilities he knew and whose weaknesses he could allow for. But Heywood was the only choice. Probably he would fail sooner or later. But the important thing was that Novoya Moskva would not think so. They were very proud of their foreigners at Central Headquarters, and of the whole over-complicated and inefficient system that supported them. They had it in their heads that a man could be a traitor to his own people and still not be crippled by the weaknesses that had driven him to treachery. Their repeated failures had done nothing to enlighten them, and for once Azarin was glad of it.

'Medical Doctor Kothu? This is Azarin. If I were to send you a suitable man – a whole man this time – could you do with him what you did with Martino?' He slapped the ends of his fingers against the edge of his desk, listening. 'That is correct. A whole man. I wish you to make me a brother for the monster. A twin.'

When he was through speaking to Kothu, Azarin called Novoya Moskva, hunching forward over his desk, his papyros jutting straight out from his hand. His jaw was firmly set, his lower teeth thrust forward past his upper jaw. His lips were stretched. His face lost its wooden blankness. It was a different sort of grin, this, from the one he usually showed the world. Like his habitual reticent mask, it had been forged in the years since he left his father's forest. Its lines on his face had been baked in by foreign suns and scoured by the sand of alien deserts. It came to him as easily, now, as the somewhat boyish smile he'd always had. The difference was that Azarin was not aware he possessed this third expression.

It took some little time to convince Central Headquarters, but Azarin felt no impatience. He hammered his plan forward like a man hewing through a tree, steadily and with measured blows, knowing that he has only to swing often enough and the tree must fall.

He hung up, finally, and drained his tea glass in a few gulps. The orderly brought more. Azarin's eyes crinkled pleasantly at the corners as he thought that once again it had been Anastas Azarin who found solutions while the clerks at Central Headquarters twittered with indecision.

He put his hand on the edge of his desk and unhurriedly pushed himself to his feet. He walked into his outer office. 'I am on my way downstairs. You will have the car waiting for me,' he told his chief clerk.

It would take the courier several days to reach Washington with Heywood's orders, but that part of the system, at least, was foolproof. Heywood would arrive here in a week. Meanwhile, there was no reason to wait for him. The cover plan was functioning automatically as of this moment. The Allieds would find Novoya Moskva much different to deal with, now that Azarin had stiffened some of the pliant spines at Central Headquarters. And, in consequence, Azarin would find his telephone much more silent, and much less peremptory.

So. Everything was arranged. By the simplest, uneducated peasant, Anastas Azarin. By the dolt who moved his lips when he read. By the tea drinker. By the ignorant man from the dark forest, who worked while Novoya Moskva talked.

Azarin's eyes twinkled as he came into Martino's room, stopped, and looked at the man. 'We will talk more,' he said. 'Now we have plenty of time to find out about the K-Eighty-eight.' It was the first time he had been able to bring the term out into the open. He saw the man's body twitch.

9

The first thing lost under these conditions, Martino discovered, was the sense of time. He was not particularly surprised, since

149

a completely foreign experience could not possibly contain any of the usual cues by which a human being learned his chronology. The room had no windows, and no clocks or calendars. These were the simplest and most obvious lacks. Then, there was no change in his routine. There was no stopping to sit down to a meal, or lying down to rest, and hunger or sleepiness furnish no help when they are constant. This room itself, somewhere in Azarin's sector headquarters, was so constructed as to offer no signposts. It was rectangular, cast in unpainted cement from floor to ceiling. Martino's route of passage was from one end to the other, and one of the walls towards which he walked was almost exactly the same as the other, even in such details as the grain of the grey surface. As he walked, he passed between two identical oak desks, facing each other, and each desk had a man in a grey-green uniform behind it. The men contrived to look alike, and a similar door entered the room behind each of them. The light fixture was exactly in the centre of the ceiling. Martino had no idea of which door he had originally used to come into the room, or towards which wall he had first marched.

As he passed the desk, it was always the man on his right who asked the first question. It might be anything: 'What is your middle name?' or 'How many inches in a foot?' The questions were meaningless, and no record was kept of his answers. The men behind the desks, who changed shifts at what might have been irregular intervals but who nevertheless always looked somehow alike, did not even care if he answered or not. If he remembered correctly, for some time at the beginning he had not answered. Somewhat later, he had irritatedly taken to giving nonsense replies: 'Newton,' or 'eight.' But now it was much less exhausting to simply tell the truth.

He knew what was happening to him. In the end, the brain in effect began manufacturing its own truth drugs in self defence against the fatigue poisons that were flooding it. The equation was: Correct replies = relief. There was none of the saving adrenalin of pain. There was only this walking through a meaningless world.

It was that last which was affecting him most strongly. The men behind the desks paid him no attention, unless he tried to

150

stop walking. The remainder of the time they simply asked their questions, looking not at him but at each other. He suspected they neither knew who he was nor cared why he was here. Lately, he had become certain of it. They were practising their trade on each other, not on him. They used him only because most two-handed games require a ball. It meant nothing to them when he began giving correct answers, because they were not here to pass judgement on his answers.

He knew they were here simply to soften him up, and that eventually Azarin would take over. But meanwhile he felt a mounting, querulous sense of terrible injustice. He was near to pouting as he walked.

He knew why that was, too. His brain, after all, had solved the problem. He was fulfilling the equation – he was doing what they wanted him to. He was giving correct answers, and by all that was reasonable, they ought to respond by giving him relief. But they ignored him; they showed no sign of understanding that he was doing what they wanted. And if he was doing what they wanted, and they ignored him, the brain could only decide that somehow it was not transmitting its signals through his actions to them. If there had been only one of them, the brain could have decided that one was deaf and blind, reciting his questions by idiotic rote. But there were two of them, always, and there must be a dozen in all. So the brain could only decide that it was he who was incapable of making himself heard – that it was Lucas Martino who was nothing.

At the same time, he knew what was happening to him.

10

Azarin sat patiently behind his desk waiting for word to come from the interrogation room. It was three days, now, since Martino had been brought from the hospital, and Azarin knew, as a man knows his trade, that the word would come sometime today.

It was quite a simple business, Azarin thought. One took a man and peeled things away from him – more vital things than skin, though he had seen that technique work at the hands of men who had not learned the subtler phases of their trade. In effect, it was much the same, though the result was cleaner. A man carries very little excess baggage in his head. Even a clerk, and a man like Martino was not a clerk. The more intelligent the man, the less excess baggage and the quicker the results. For once you exposed the man underneath, he was raw and tender – a touch here and there, and he gave up what he knew.

Of course, having done that and knowing he had done that, the man was empty thereafter. He had found himself to be pliable, and after that anyone could use him – could do anything he wanted with him. He bore the mark of whoever touched him last. He did what you wanted of him. He was a living nothing.

Ordinarily, Azarin drew only a normal measure of satisfaction from having done this to a man while he himself remained, for ever and imperishable, Anastas Azarin. But in this case –

Azarin growled at something invisible across the room.

Chapter 15

Eddie Bates was a sleeper. He was a wiry, flat-bellied, ugly man with a face that had been grotesquely scarred by acne. His youth had been miserable, for all that he faithfully lifted weights a half-hour every day in his bedroom. Towards the end of his teens he had spent six months in a reformatory for assault and battery. It should have been assault with intent to kill, but only Eddie knew how far he had planned to go when he first began hitting the other boy – a flashily good-looking youngster who had made a remark about a girl Eddie never had found the courage to speak to.

When he was twenty, he found a job in a garage. He worked in a mood of perpetual sullen resentment that made most of the customers dislike him. Only one of them – a casually likeable man who drove an expensive car – had taken pains to cultivate his friendship. Eddie ran a few errands for him after work, and assumed he was a criminal of some kind, since he paid quite well and had Eddie deliver his cryptic messages by roundabout methods.

Eddie did his work well and faithfully, tied to the man by something more than money. The man was the only respectable friend he had in the world, and when the man made him another offer, Eddie accepted.

So, Eddie Bates had become a sleeper. His friend now paid him not to run messages, and to stay out of trouble. He found him a job as an airlines mechanic. Every month that Eddie continued to be a respectable citizen, and drew his pay from the airline, an envelope with additional pay reached him by means as devious as those in which Eddie had once been employed. By now, Eddie knew who his friend was working for.

But the man was his friend, and he was never asked to do anything else to earn the extra money.

Eddie avoided considering the realities of his position. As time went by, this became progressively easier.

He grew older, and continued to work for the airline. Several things happened to him. For one thing, he had a natural talent for machinery. He understood it, respected it, and was willing to work with infinite patience until it was functioning properly. He found that very few of the people he worked with turned away from his face once they had seen him work on an engine. For another, he had found a girl.

Alice worked in the diner where Eddie ate his lunch every day. She was a hard-working girl who knew that the only kind of man worth bothering with was a steady man with a good trade. Looks were not particularly important to her – she distrusted handsome men on principle. It was an accepted thing between her and Eddie that they would be married as soon as they had enough money saved for the down payment on a house near the airport.

But now Eddie Bates, the sleeper, had been activated. He crouched near the plane's inboard engine nacelle, up on the high wing far above the dark hanger floor, and wondered what he was going to do.

He had his orders. He had more – he had the thing his friend had given him. It was a metal cartridge the size of a pint milk bottle, one end of which was a knob with time calibrations marked off on it. His friend had preset it and given it to him, and told him to put it in an engine. He had not explained that it was only intended to force the plane down into the water at a pre-calculated point. Eddie assumed it was meant to blow the wing off in flight. He was a mechanic, not an explosives expert. Like most people, he had no accurate idea of the power of a given weight of charge, and no idea how much of the cartridge's actual bulk was taken up by timing mechanisms.

He wavered for a long time, hidden by himself in the darkness near the hangar roof. He added things up time after time, growing more desperate and more indecisive.

He had never quite expected that he would be asked to do something like this. He gradually admitted to himself that as

154

time had gone by, he had come to believe that he would never be asked to do anything. But the man was his friend, and Eddie had taken his money.

But he had other friends, now, and he had worked on this engine himself this afternoon, tuning it patiently.

But the money was important. It was helping his savings a great deal. The more he saved, the sooner he could marry Alice. But if he didn't plant the bomb, the money would stop.

Other things might happen if he didn't plant the bomb. His friend might turn him in somehow, and then he would lose the respect of his friends here in the shop, and never marry Alice.

He had to do something.

He drew a quick breath and thrust the bomb through the opened inspection plate into the space between the engine and the inner surface of the nacelle. He hastily bolted the plate back down and ran out of the hangar.

He had done only one thing to offset the complete helplessness he felt. As he slipped the cartridge through the opened inspection plate, his fingers closed on it convulsively, almost as though by reflex, almost as though clutching at some hope of salvation, or almost as though thrusting away something precious to him. And he knew as he was doing it that it was only an empty gesture, because what did it matter when the plane crashed?

He had re-set the timer, but no one – certainly not Eddie Bates – could have said by how much.

Chapter 16

I must remember, Martino thought, looking across the office at Colonel Azarin, that the K-Eighty-eight is not meant to be a bribe. Some people buy the attention of other people by telling them things. No man is so drab as not to have some personal detail that will intrigue others. I must remember that I can tell Azarin about the time I played hookey from grammar school because I was ashamed to raise my hand to go to the washroom. That is intriguing enough, and will attract enough attention to me. Or I can tell him some back fence gossip – about Johnson, the astrophysicist, for instance, who looks at figure studies in his room at night. That will hold his attention at least until I have exhausted all the details of the story. I can tell him all these things, and as many more as I can remember, but I must not try to hold his attention by telling him about the K-Eighty-eight because that is not a proper use of it.

I must remember, he thought with infinite patience for clarity's sake, never to admit I know anything about the K-Eighty-eight. That is the greatest defence against the urge to gossip – to look surprised or pretend disinterest when someone comes to you for further details.

'Sit down, Doctor of Science Martino,' Azarin said, smiling pleasantly. 'Please be so good.'

Martino felt the answering smile well up through his entire body. He felt the traitor joy begin as a faint surprise that someone had spoken to him at last, and then spread into a great warmth at this man who called him by name.

Not thinking that nothing would show on his face, he trembled with panic at the thought of how easily Azarin was breaking through his defences. He had hoped to be stronger than this.

156

I must remember to say *nothing*, he thought, urgently now. If ever I begin, my friendship for this man won't let me stop. I have to fight to say nothing at all.

'Would you care for a cigarette?' Azarin extended the sandalwood box across the desk.

Martino's right hand was trembling. He reached with his left. The metal fingertips, badly controlled, broke the papyros to shreds.

He saw Azarin frown for the moment, and in that moment Martino almost cried out, he was so upset by what he had done to offend this man. But it took an effort to activate the proper vocal affectors in his brain, and his brain detected it and stopped it.

I must remember I have other friends, he thought. I must remember that Edith and Barbara will be killed if I please this friend.

He realized in a panic that Edith and Barbara were not his friends any longer – that they probably did not remember him – that no one remembered or noticed him or cared about him except Azarin.

I must remember, he thought. I must remember to apologize to Edith and Barbara if I ever leave here. I must remember I will leave here.

Azarin was smiling. 'A glass of tea?'

I must think about that, he thought. If I take tea, I will have to open my mouth. If I do that, will I be able to close it again?

'Don't be afraid, Doctor of Science Martino. Everything is all right now. We will sit, and we will talk, and I will listen to you.'

He felt himself beginning to do it. I must remember not going to school – and Johnson, he thought frantically.

Why? he wondered.

Because the K-Eighty-eight is not meant to be a bribe.

What does that mean?

He listened to himself think in fascination, absorbed by this phenomenon of two opposing drives in a single mechanism, and wondered just exactly how his mind did the trick – what kind of circuits were involved, and were they actually in operation simultaneously or did they use the same components alternately.

'Are you playing with me?' Azarin shouted. 'What are you doing, behind that face? Are you *laughing* at me?'

Martino stared at Azarin in surprise. What? What had he done?

He could not wonder how long it might take him to complete a train of thought. It did not seem to him that a very long time at all had gone by since Azarin's last question, or that a man looking at him might see nothing but an implacable, graven-faced figure with a deadly metal arm lying quiet but always ready to crush.

'Martino, I did not bring you here for comedies!' Azarin's eyes suddenly narrowed. Martino thought he saw fear under the anger, and it puzzled him greatly. 'Did Rogers plan this? Did he *deliberately* send you?'

Martino began to shake his head, to try to explain. But he caught himself. The thought began to come to him that there was no need to talk to this man – that he had already attracted all of Azarin's attention.

The telephone rang, with the hard, shrill insistence that always came when the switchboard operator was relaying a call from Novoya Moskva.

Azarin picked it up and listened.

Martino watched him with no curiosity while Azarin's eyes opened wide. After a time, Azarin put the phone down, and Martino still took no notice. Even when Azarin's shrunken voice muttered, 'Your college friend, Heywood, drowned six hundred miles too soon,' Martino had no notion of what it meant.

2

Martino sat motionless in the Tatra as it drew near the border. The S.I.B. man beside him – an Asiatic named Yung –was too quick to interpret every movement as an opening to practise his conversational English.

Three months wasted, Martino was thinking. The whole programme must be bogged down. I only hope they haven't tried to rebuild that particular configuration.

He searched his mind for the modified system he was almost certain he had thought of in their hospital. He had been trying

158

to bring it back for the past two weeks, while Kothu and a therapist worked on him. But he had not been able to quite grasp it. Several times he thought he had it, but the memory was patchy and useless.

Well, he thought as the car stopped, the therapist told me there was bound to be some trouble for a while. But it'll come to me.

'Here you are, Doctor Martino,' Yung said brightly, unsnapping the door.

'Yes.' He looked out at the gateway, with its Soviet guards. Beyond it, he could see the Allied soldiers, and a car with two men getting out of it.

He began to walk towards them. There'll be problems, he reminded himself. These people aren't used to my looks. It'll take a while to overcome that.

But it can be done. A man is something more than just a collection of features. And I'll get to work soon. That'll keep me busy. If I can't remember that idea I had in the hospital, I can always work out something else.

It's been a bad time, he thought, stepping through the gate. But I haven't lost anything.

Penguin Science Fiction

The following books of 'SF' are available in Penguins:

*AVAILABLE IN THE U.S.A.

*For a complete list of books available please write to Penguin Books
whose address can be found on the back of the title page*